MW00475257

TEN CENT BILL

THE INSPIRING TRUE STORY OF ONE MAN'S EPIC JOURNEY FROM SLAVERY TO GREATNESS.

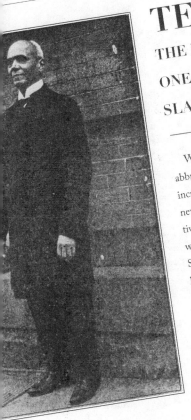

MACON, GEORGIA, DECEMBER 21ST, 1919

TEN CENT BILL

THE INSPIRING TRUE STORY OF ONE MAN'S EPIC JOURNEY FROM SLAVERY TO GREATNESS.

When I first stumbled across the abbreviated chronicle of Bill Yopp's incredible life in a yellowing old newspaper article I was totally captivated by the story of this man who was born into slavery in the American South and rose to greatness through his hard work, kindness to others, and generosity. His boundless sense of adventure and his ability to achieve goals far beyond the reach of others with his background also fascinated me. As I learned more about him I quickly realized that his remarkable story needed to be told because of the it can teach us all. Never come across a person who in material wealth or e was able to positively im lives. Thus began a four bits and pieces of his and 90 year old abbre of his life and a multi per articles spread ac United States.

Continued page

WRITTEN BY
CHARLES PITTMAN

TATE PUBLISHING & Enterprises

Ten Cent Bill: The Inspiring True Story of One's Man Epic Journey from Slavery to Greatness.
Copyright © 2008 by Charles Pittman. All rights reserved.

This title is also available as a Tate Out Loud product. Visit www.tatepublishing.com for more information.

No part of this publication may be reproduced, stored in a retrieval system or transmitted in any way by any means, electronic, mechanical, photocopy, recording or otherwise without the prior permission of the author except as provided by USA copyright law.

This novel is a work of fiction. However, several names, descriptions, entities, and incidents included in the story are based on the lives of real people.

The opinions expressed by the author are not necessarily those of Tate Publishing, LLC.

Published by Tate Publishing & Enterprises, LLC
127 E. Trade Center Terrace | Mustang, Oklahoma 73064 USA
1.888.361.9473 | www.tatepublishing.com

Tate Publishing is committed to excellence in the publishing industry. The company reflects the philosophy established by the founders, based on Psalm 68:11,
"The Lord gave the word and great was the company of those who published it."

Book design copyright © 2008 by Tate Publishing, LLC. All rights reserved.
Cover design by Leah LeFlore
Interior design by Kandi Evans

Published in the United States of America
ISBN: 978-1-60696-296-1

1. Fiction: Historical
2. Biography & Autobiography: People of Color
09.01.05

DEDICATION

This book would not be possible without the loving support of my wife, Mallery, who after thirty–two years of love is still my strength and purpose in life. You have always supported my writing, patiently listened to my ideas, accompanied me on research trips, and believed in me. I love you, Mallery, and will forever.

I also dedicate this book to my mother and father. Dad gave me the model on which I have based my life, and Mom gave me her love for history, a passion for story telling, and the inspiration to express my feelings with written words. I know they would be proud, which was always my goal.

INTRODUCTION

When I first stumbled across the abbreviated chronicle of Bill Yopp's incredible life in a yellowing newspaper article, I was completely captivated by the story of this man. Born into slavery in the American South, he rose to greatness through his hard work, kindness to others, and generosity. His boundless sense of adventure and his ability to achieve goals beyond the reach of most blacks during this period of history also fascinated me. I quickly realized that his story needed to be told because of the life lessons it can teach us all. Never before had I come across a person who had so little in material wealth or education and yet positively impacted so many lives. Thus began a four year search for bits and pieces of his legacy from ninety–year–old abbreviated accounts of his life and a multitude of newspaper articles spread across most of the United States.

Ten Cent Bill is the story of an antebellum slave who accompanied his best friend, his white master's son, onto the horrible battlefields of the Civil War. Upon achieving his freedom from slavery, he achieved prominence on his own during the early twentieth century.

Ten Cent Bill reveals the life of this extraordinary man who overcame unimaginable prejudices to become highly respected in his home state of Georgia. He achieved this high level of esteem partly because of his unselfish dedication to a small group of destitute, elderly Confederate comrades who were living in a state run old soldier's home in Atlanta.

Between 1870 and 1930, Bill's newfound freedom carried him around the world to over thirty countries. He rubbed elbows with powerful politicians and millionaires, dined with royalty, and single-handedly influenced the Georgia State Legislature to establish pensions for Civil War veterans housed in the Georgia Confederate Soldier's Home in Atlanta.

I chose to write this book as a historical novel, which enabled me to better tell the extraordinary story of his life and build Bill's personality as I have interpreted it. I have endeavored to keep the timeline for this story as accurate as the information on his life would allow while using my knowledge of Southern history to build the characters and the plot. The primary events and accomplishments depicted here are true. Some characters and events are fictitious and were woven into the story to give a better feel for the era in which Bill Yopp lived. While I have attempted to keep relationship information as accurate as possible, some character names and dates related to them are educated guesses based upon intensive genealogy research.

As you will discover while reading this story, Bill's life represented love, compassion, honesty, dignity, unselfishness, and dedication—a rare combination of qualities for anyone, especially for someone who began his life as the property of another man.

GOD WAS IN THEIR MIDST TODAY

JUNE 7, 1936
CONFEDERATE MILITARY CEMETERY
MARIETTA, GEORGIA

The torrential late night thunderstorm that swept through the city had left the ground soggy and the morning air uncommonly cool for early June. Thick pockets of wispy ground fog still obscured most of the creek bottoms in the sprawling cemetery, but the haze on the gently rolling hills was quickly clearing in the morning sun. Near the front of the graveyard, an unusually large assembly of silent dark–suited people was gathered on a tree–covered hill to offer their last respects to a departed old soldier. As they stood in reverent groups around the open grave, rays of sunlight shot like golden arrows through misty gaps in the oak canopy and made more than one person sense that God was in their midst today. Row upon row of white marble headstones, all the same size and shape, spread out across the hills and produced a feeling of quiet reverence and awe. Even the most talkative of the spectators found themselves whispering in the presence of these fallen brothers as if concerned that they would disturb their peaceful sleep.

The mourners grew suddenly quiet as the faint, eerie sound of a lone drummer rattling out the ageless beat of a funeral march penetrated the morning silence. Curious heads turned left and right as the group searched for a glimpse of the musician while the sound echoed around the knolls and through the valleys. No one knew quite where it was. Several seconds had passed when a young drummer dressed in a gray Confederate soldier's uniform materialized, ghostlike, from a wall of fog a hundred yards away. He marched slowly toward the gathering group, his old drum swaying back and forth on its neck strap while he drummed out the monotonous death beat. A few seconds later, the distinctive sounds of horse hooves clopping on the granite–cobbled road were heard, and straight away everyone saw the animals and their gray–suited riders as they too emerged from the mist directly behind the drummer.

Three pairs of dark brown horses with black bridles pulled a black caisson on which a flag draped coffin rested. The front half of the coffin was covered with an American flag and on the back laid the Confederate flag. Three men, also dressed in gray uniforms, sat atop three of the horses while seven rifle wielding soldiers in Confederate uniforms marched slowly behind the caisson in perfect step to the drum beat.

No one said a word as the soldiers removed the heavy coffin from the open wagon and carefully carried it the twenty paces to the empty grave where they placed it on a small fabric draped platform. Several large arrangements of red, white, and blue flowers with colorful ribbons made a fitting backdrop for the flag covered casket.

The drumming stopped.

The gathering included many of Atlanta's most powerful politicians, including the Governor of Georgia, the mayor, a handful of senators, and several state representatives. In another group, several publishers and editors from prestigious Georgia newspapers stood together. Several ribbon encrusted generals from Fort McPherson, an army base just south of Atlanta, stood with their arms crossed in reverence. Also in attendance was Marion Ramsey, the influential Superintendent of the Central of Georgia Railroad. Several dozen ordinary people, both blacks and whites, stood together on the hillside and watched the proceedings. Many people held hands to comfort each other. The sounds of muffled sobs, sniffling, and blowing noses could be heard throughout the group of mourners.

A dozen elderly men wearing colorful war medals on their chests slowly took their seats on the front row of chairs nearest the coffin. Most of these men wore dark suits and used walking canes while several others were in wheel chairs. A few were missing an arm or leg. They were the last residents of the Georgia Confederate Soldier's Home and were there to say farewell to one of their own fallen heroes. His name was Bill Yopp, more affectionately known as Ten Cent Bill. Each person in attendance could tell dozens of stories of how Bill Yopp, a former slave, had touched their lives in positive and meaningful ways.

Several of the frail old warriors stared glassy–eyed at Bill's coffin and the Confederate flag while others could not take their eyes off the men dressed in the Confederate uniforms who stood behind it. For several of them, this was the first time in over seventy years that they had seen a Confederate soldier except in their dreams or nightmares.

Each of these survivors had experienced the horrors of the bloodiest war in American history. Some had attended the funerals of deceased Confederate generals and other high-ranking officers, but no one had witnessed such a large group of mourners or a ceremony with such military pomp as this one. The fact that Bill Yopp had been a lowly Confederate drummer boy and never rose above the rank of private was a testament to the importance this man held in their memories.

A distinguished robed minister who had known Bill well stepped out of the crowd and stood beside the coffin. He was noticeably emotional and cleared his throat several times before he spoke. After a few words of welcome to everyone, he recited a short and meaningful prayer that wished Private Bill Yopp a safe journey to heaven and thanked the Lord for sharing this man with the world. As the fog lifted that morning, there was little doubt in anyone's mind that Bill's spirit rose with it.

When the minister completed his remarks, the Superintendent of the Confederate Soldier's Home, Major John McAllister, stepped forward and told special stories about the slave from Georgia who had fought for the Confederacy during the Civil War. He described the life of the small black man who had traveled around

the world, rubbed elbows with some of the most powerful people in America, and had become one of the most
well respected men in the state. In closing, McAllister
described how Bill had accomplished these feats at a time
when most black people in America continued to be considered second class citizens by the majority of the white
population.

—

When the ceremony concluded, most of the attendees
walked slowly by Bill's casket to wish him a fond farewell.
A ninety–five-year-old soldier hobbled up to Bill's flag
draped coffin, stood upright at stiff attention, and gave
a crisp salute. "Here's to you, Bill. You take care of them
boys up in heaven like you did us, and we'll be there soon
to see you again. I'll miss you, my old friend, Ten Cent
Bill."

I'LL BE THE HARMONY TO EVERY SONG YOU SING

According to scanty records, the summer of 1845 in Laurens County Georgia was one of the hottest of the decade. By mid–day the temperature would rise to one hundred degrees or more and the humidity was so thick that, according some old timers, the houseflies would get stuck in mid air and drown from the moisture.

It was on a day such as this in July of 1845 that William H. Yopp, Jr. was born into slavery on a sprawling plantation named Whitehall. The plantation was owned by a man named Jeremiah Yopp, who was described as a big man with a smart head on his shoulders. He was also known for his fair minded and sympathetic attitudes toward the slaves who worked and lived on his farms. Partially due to his father's brilliance and wealth, Jeremiah was able to build upon his successes at farming and ultimately owned two large plantations in Laurens County. Each plantation was successful because of the large numbers of slaves they owned and Jeremiah's excellent management.

Bill was one of the lucky slaves, if there could be such a description, because his parents were the house servants for the Yopp family. This meant that as a child he spent most of his days in the luxury of the plantation kitchen house, where his mother, Helia Yopp, worked as the chief cook. Rather than being fed a diet of field greens, grits, and an occasional piece of meat, he would eat what their Master ate. And rather than being put to work in the fields as a child, he wore clean clothes and did chores for his master.

Helia, whose nickname was Lia, was a portly woman who had a reputation as one of the best cooks in the county and was often asked to train cooks who belonged to other plantations. She also made it her life's ambition to teach each of her children how to cook and cook well. Her reasoning was that there would always be a place for a good cook, and she meant for all of her children to "have a place."

It was said when Lia was preparing one of her special Sunday dinners, Master Yopp would make it a habit of coming to the kitchen for a sample two or three times before the meal was served. One of her specialties was her egg custard that was said to be as smooth and sweet as a kiss from your sweetheart. Lia was said to have a pleasant personality and thoroughly enjoyed laughing and singing. In spite of her hard days working in the hot kitchen, she managed to put a grin on the face of anyone who spent time with her.

Bill's father was William Yopp, Sr., who had been "assigned" his last name when he was bought by Jeremiah. All slaves owned by a plantation took on the last name of their owner primarily as a method to distinguish them from slaves owned by other plantations. This naming practice also had practical business applications. When a slave was sent into town to pick up a wagon load of supplies, he simply told the store owner his name, and it was clear who would be responsible for payment. It also meant that when a slave ran away he could easily be returned to his rightful owner by simply knowing his full name.

William was born in South Carolina and was sold to the Yopps as a teenager in the early 1800s. His easy–going style, hard work, and excellent manners soon landed him a job working in Jeremiah's stables. Several years later, he was promoted to work in the main house as a butler. He was a handsome man, with smooth light brown skin, and he walked very erect.

Bill was the fourth of seven children born to William and Lia. He was born in a dirt floored slave shanty that was less than fifty yards from the kitchen building. Two days after the birth, Lia was back at work in the Yopp kitchen.

Bill recalled later in his life that his early years at Whitehall Plantation were some of the most pleasant of his life. He often reminisced about events, such as the night he and his cousins had a hankering for some fresh corn. On this especially dark night, they sneaked into a small cornfield and pulled up ten or fifteen stalks that were on the ends of the rows. They proceeded to strip the fat ears of corn from the stalks and had the biggest corn roast of their lives. By getting the corn stalks from the ends of the rows, they could brush over the ground to make it look like nothing had ever been there. It was better than pulling up stalks in the middle of the rows and leaving gaps.

The following day, the plantation overseer came to the shanty of Bill's cousin and asked him if he thought this particular cornfield was getting smaller. His cousin looked the overseer straight in the eyes without cracking a smile and said, "Boss man, I been noticin' that too, but it ain't that the field is getting smaller. It's the woods next to the field that is shrinkin' back. I believe that the beavers have been eatin' the trees, and the caterpillars are eatin' all the leaves. It jes make that corn field look smaller." The overseer scratched his head and rode off not knowing what to make of the mystery of the shrinking woods. Bill said that he and his cousins laughed so hard that they were crying and rolling in the grass like an old heifer in a dusting pit.

Bill also reminisced in his older years about all of the hard work that the slave women in the main house performed each day. Two women ran the big weaving room that the Yopps had built onto the back of their home. There were several flocks of sheep on Whitehall and plenty of cotton. What wool and cotton was not sold at market was made into blankets and clothing items. When Bill was a small child, he would sit in this weaving room and watch in amazement as the women ran the looms. He talked of watching how fast the women could make the shuttles fly in and out carrying a long tail of brightly colored thread. Jokingly, Bill said that the older he got, the more tired he grew of listening to the women talk all day. He said, "If the Lawd had said that they couldn't talk for a month, I believe they would have shriveled up and died like a frog on a hot rock."

The Yopps also had another large room for carding and spinning, and this was the room where most of the singing was done. Bill remembered a lady, known as Mammy Jane, who ran this room, and she knew more about dyeing than anyone else around. She knew what kinds of roots, leaves, and berries made green, blue, red, or orange…just about any color in the rainbow. She had big, old, black dye pots out under a shed, and one of Bill's least pleasant memories was hauling wood and stoking the fires for these dye pots. Old Mammy Jane was like a scientist. She knew right when to pour in the vinegar and the salt to set the colors, and she knew right when to yank them out to dry. Bill said he always liked to go out to the clothesline and see Mammy Jane's Rainbow hanging and drying after the day's work was done. One good thing that came from all of the spinning and sewing was that at Christmas, the lady of the house, Margaret Yopp, would give every one of the slaves a new pair of wool socks.

Bill recalled his early days as a long, pleasant recollection of playing with the other boys and girls, both black and white, and doing whatever chores his mama or daddy thought he could do without creating problems. He joked about hauling water buckets to the horse troughs 'til his arms stretched. But his most pleasant memories were of spending time with Jeremiah's youngest son, Thomas. When Bill was born, Thomas was already seventeen years old. By the time Bill was seven or eight years old, Jeremiah "gave" Bill to Thomas to be his personal servant and fishing companion. Little did they know at that time that their friendship and dedication to each other would span the next seventy years.

Thomas Yopp was a spindly young man who always had a smile on his face and got his daddy's smartness and his mother's gentle nature. His favorite pastimes were fishing and hunting. Bill recalled getting up early in the morning and digging worms, and shortly after daylight, they would be down on the river "drowning the worms" in search of a big fish. They had many wonderful days floating along the river in their old flat-bottomed cypress board boat that Bill's father had built years earlier for Jeremiah. The two boys would catch so many fish that during the spring and summer they could feed nearly the whole farm on a Saturday night with what they caught that day. Bill's mother would cook up a heaping kettle of fried hushpuppies to go with the fish, and Bill never forgot her recipes.

Another tale told frequently by Bill was about the times when he and Thomas would go out to shoot some Bob White quail for dinner. Their favorite method of hunting was to go to the corncrib, get a gunny sack full of dried yellow corn, and haul it out to the edge of the field that was frequented by these elusive birds. Bill would take the old hand plow and dig a deep furrow about twenty feet long, and then he would sprinkle the corn down the furrow. When that was finished, they would build a blind from limbs and vines at the end of the furrow and wait for the quail to come for their afternoon meal. Bill was especially proud of his ability to whistle like a quail and said that as soon as he would start calling them they would call back. It wouldn't take long for the birds to find the corn, and they would line up in that furrow so thickly that it looked like a long feathery snake. Bill said that they would be so quiet that "you could've heard a mouse fart." About that time, you'd hear 'kaboom!' Thomas would fire one shot with his big shotgun right down the length of that furrow, and he'd kill fifteen or twenty all with one shot.

—

As the years passed, young Bill's relationship with Thomas flourished. Bill was quoted as saying, "Masr Thomas and I were like 'Mary had a little lamb.' Wherever the Masr went, I was sure to go." Through all of this, a real affection grew between the two in spite of the difference in their ages and the color of their skin. Bill looked upon Thomas with admiration and respect, and Thomas treated Bill with consideration and kindness.

It was obvious during Bill's childhood that until he was about ten or eleven years old, he didn't realize there was a real difference between the white children and him other than the color of their skin. Up to that time, if the white children got to eat, then he got to eat. If they got to go swimming, the he got to go too. They were just like one big family of Yopps. But things began to change for

Bill when he grew old enough to start doing some serious work for Thomas and his father. That's when he learned that there really was a difference between him and the white children, and it made him truly sad. He later said that it hurt his heart for a long time when Jeremiah would ask him to do some chores that he wouldn't ask the white children to do. If the dog messed on the floor, he was the one who had to clean it up. Thomas and the other white children never touched anything as filthy as this...only the black children.

Bill recollected the night he cried himself to sleep after telling his parents about those feelings. They tried to console him and help him understand that that was the life the Lord had given him and he just had to make the best of it. Bill's father told him on more than one occasion, "Bill, if you goin' to be contented in this white man's world, then you gots to learn what makes the white man happy and do as he says. Yo life will be much better that way. If'n you try to buck the work and you make the white man angry, then he can take away everything that matters to you."

William constantly reminded Bill that they lived a good life compared to the field slaves. These field hands got up at sunrise and worked hard until sunset almost every day, even when it was so hot one could barely breathe. They were usually so tired and worn out at night that they could barely eat supper before falling asleep. Then they would get up and do it all again the next day.

Bill could remember the workers singing lots on

Sundays, which was their day off from work. Generally they were a happy bunch because they knew that their lives could be even worse on some of the other plantations. He had heard stories that some of the slaves who had worked on other plantations were whipped by their overseers if they broke the rules or didn't work hard enough. Bill's father told him about several slaves he had known who had been scarred so badly by beatings that their backs looked like snakes had crawled under their skin. But this never happened on Master Jeremiah's place. On most days, Jeremiah and Thomas would be out in the fields with the slaves and would even bring them water and help them with certain chores. Jeremiah seemed to really care for them as long as they did their jobs and weren't lazy about it.

It was told that during the middle of the summer when the field hands were harvesting tobacco or corn, sometimes Jeremiah or Thomas would tell everyone to stop working for a while and go swimming in the creek. It was obvious that these slave owners realized that if the field hands could take an occasional break and cool off, they wouldn't get sick. In turn, he would get more work out of them with fewer problems.

Bill especially enjoyed telling the story about his experiences one summer when he worked with the field slaves, something unheard of for house servants unless they were being punished for some breach of faith with the master. Bill recounted that he literally begged Thomas to be allowed to join his friends in the field and help with the tobacco harvest that particular summer. Nobody could understand why he would want to do this and thought that perhaps he had been sneaking sips of his master's brandy at the ripe age of thirteen.

Eventually everyone learned that he simply wanted the experience so that his friends would no longer tease him about being "only" a house servant. When his friends would talk about driving the mule sled through the fields, or pulling the green leaves and stuffing them under their left arm until they could not hold anymore, or hanging the tobacco stakes up in the curing barns, Bill wanted to be able to say that he knew what that was like.

Bill thought he knew what hard work and heat would be like, but he was in for the surprise of his life that late July when the tobacco began to ripen. Thomas had pulled the overseer to the side and told him to make certain that Bill was allowed to fully appreciate the tobacco harvest. He didn't intend this as any punishment: he just wanted him to taste the rough life. Bill soon found out that hanging the long wooden stakes laced with heavy green tobacco leaves twenty–five feet off the ground in the tops of curing barns was what changed boys into men. When it was ninety degrees outside, they could count on it being one hundred and ten degrees in the ceilings of those tall barns. If the heat wasn't enough to contend with, the stinging tobacco sap that plastered their arms and the fact that they did all of this while balancing barefoot on rough–hewn boards far above the hard dirt floor would do the trick.

During his first three days in the barns, Bill became exhausted by noon and was on the verge of collapsing. Each time he felt shaky and saw stars floating in his eyes, he would rest for fifteen minutes, drink lots of cool water, and pour ladles of water over his head. This would revive him, and he was able to finish out the day. After balancing on the wooden beams for several hours, his feet became so sore that he could hardly walk.

When it was finally over, though, he felt an uplifting sense of pride that this "house boy" could keep up with his leather–handed slave friends. He also began to understand that there were good jobs to have, and there were the better ones. He knew after that summer that he would be thankful for what he had. He began focusing his efforts on working harder in order to be the best at what he did. He never wanted anything to happen that could jeopardize his life in the big house with Thomas.

Bill often recalled one of his fondest memories of childhood when his mother would hold him in her lap, sitting in the old rocking chair out under oaks late in the evening. As he grew older, by the end of each day he would have a head full of questions about why they lived one way and the master lived another. Bill and his parents would sit and talk or sing almost every night until, as Bill remembered, "the lightnin' bugs stopped blinking and the old hoot owl started callin' for his sweetheart."

On many of those nights, Jeremiah and Thomas would come out to the slave quarters, have a seat with the slaves, and tell stories of places they had been or seen or read about. Lots of evenings they would build big fires in the pit, and old men would tell stories to the children and sing. Throughout the remainder of Bill's life, whenever he was feeling down or lonely, he would find himself singing one of his favorite childhood songs called 'Possum Up the Gum Stump'. It went like this:

> Possum up the gum stump
> The raccoon's in the holler
> Twist him out and get him down
> And I'll give you half a dollar.
> Possum up the gum stump
> Yes, cooney's in the holler
> A pretty girl goes down my house
> Just as fast as she can waller.
> Possum up the gum stump
> His jaw is black and dirty
> To come and kiss you, pretty girl
> I'd run like a gobbler turkey.

Bill never forgot one of the last times he ever sat down and sang songs with his mother. It was just before he left for the war. She pulled him tight to her body with a big hug and said, "Bill, whenever you sing our favorite songs, no matter where you are, I want you to remember that I'll always be the harmony to every song you sing. Whenever you are sad, just sing our songs and remember that I'll be in the back part of your mind singing with you and tellin' you to smile. Jes remember your old Mama and the good times we had singin' together."

FORTY ACRES AND A MULE

1859

Bill was about fourteen years old when he first heard some talk that folks in the South might split away from the North. None of this really mattered to Bill or the other slaves until they started hearing that one of the promises the Yankees were making was that there would be no more slavery. Everyone would be free to live where they wanted to live and work where they wanted to work.

Sitting around the campfire one night in early 1861, an older slave who had just returned from a wagon trip into Dublin, Georgia, told everyone about meeting a black man who was free. This freedman had told him that he was from New York, where they had outlawed slavery and all black people were free as birds. It didn't take long for this story to spread like wildfire through the slave quarters, and it stirred up a hornet's nest. Everyone wanted to know about the free black man and what his life was like.

It didn't take Jeremiah and Thomas very long to get wind of this freedom talk going around in the slave quarters, so they came down to the campfire one night to talk with everyone about what was happening. All of the slaves from the entire plantation gathered around the fire, and one could have heard a pin drop as Jeremiah climbed up on the back of a wagon to talk to them.

The orange fire made Jeremiah's eyes shine like black marbles as he scanned the gathering crowd. The mothers held their babies on their hips, and the older kids chased the dogs or drew circles in the dirt as their master began talking.

Jeremiah cleared his throat and began.

"I think all of you know that we have built a plantation that is a good home for all of us," he said in his deep, booming voice.

"I try to do all I can to help you, and Miss Margaret and I always wish we could do more. As you can see, my family doesn't live any kind of fancy life like many plantation owners do. We work in the fields alongside you almost every day. That's because we have always tried to share as much of our food and clothing with you as possible. I'm guessing you get twice as much food as most slaves in this county, and we give all of you new clothes at least once a year. And most importantly, we always try to listen to you when you have problems."

Jeremiah turned to face Bill's father who was standing near the wagon.

"William," he said as he turned to him. "When your brother got sick over on Bill Puckett's farm, I let you go over there for two days to be with him. I even gave you a horse to ride and a dollar to buy some food. I have done the same kind of thing for several of you, but we don't need to get into all of that tonight. Just understand that we care about all of you."

Jeremiah paused and stared down at the glowing fire. The look on his face was worrisome and serious.

"I know that you have been hearing some talk and rumors about the Southern states splitting off from the North because the Yankees want to do away with slavery. Some of the stories you are hearing are true, and some of them are not. What has been happening is that the Northern states elected a man named Abraham Lincoln to be president of the United States, and not a single Southern state voted for him. Lincoln and his Republican party have pledged to the Yankees that their primary job will be to stop the growth of slavery. I can understand what he is saying to a point. Perhaps we shouldn't allow slavery to expand beyond where it is currently. But if those Yankees try to come down here and tell all of us that we can't run our farms the way we want to, the way we have to, then you all will be out of a home and a place to live and raise your families. Yes, you would get your freedom, but you would all have to move to the big cities up North to get decent jobs. I don't think any of you want to do that. Our Southern cities don't have many factories and businesses to give all of you jobs since the South's business is almost totally based on farming."

"Your other option would be to go buy your own place and start farming on your own." Jeremiah paused and looked around at the hushed faces. Not expecting any replies, he asked, "How many of you here have enough money to go buy forty acres and a mule and everything it takes to run a farm?"

Jeremiah explained that on January 16, 1861, he had attended the Convention of Succession at the Georgia capitol of Milledgeville. Some people of Laurens County had agreed to side with the Cooperationists who wanted to remain in the Union, but he had voted with the majority to secede from the Union.

He looked slowly around at the dark faces and bright white eyes that glowed in the firelight and didn't hear a word from anyone. The cool night air was thick with nervousness and fear. The only sound was the eerie howl of a hound dog chasing a raccoon back in the woods behind the houses.

"If the day ever comes when the government says that all slaves can be free, then I'll be the first one to open the front gate and see you on your way to freedom. But you need to know that freedom is not all it is promised to be. There's a lot of responsibility and danger all wrapped up with it that is hard to see from where you are standing."

One of the older black men standing around the fire stepped forward. Joseph was about fifty–five years old with gray hair and stood there barefooted with ragged pants and a loose shirt. He was a respected man in the quarters.

"Masr Jeremiah, there is two things you have said that I agree with. First, I agrees that you have been a good Masr to us. And next, I agrees that nobody in this camp can afford to buy his own farm. If we gets freed by Masr

Lincoln, then can't we jes stay here with you and have you pay us a fair wage to work the farm for you?"

Yopp pulled his hands behind his back and locked his fingers together as he stared over at the flaming fire pit. He could sense the hopelessness and fear in the black man's voice. The night was turning colder, and he noticed that each time he exhaled, a small smoky cloud blew into the evening air.

"Joseph," Jeremiah called out calmly, "I've known you for almost thirty years. Have I ever lied to you about anything? Have I?"

The old black man shook his head and said, "Naw, suh. You never has. You has always been straight up with me and I 'preciate it."

"The problem I have … let me restate that," Yopp said as he shifted his weight to his other leg. "The problem we all have is that there just isn't enough money produced on this farm to pay the number of folks that it takes to farm it. Between the slaves and my family, we have over forty folks living here. I could probably afford to give half of you decent jobs, but with the smaller number of workers we would be producing less money. I couldn't afford to pay everybody but a half fair wage. It's a real worrisome predicament," he said as he shook his head and looked at all of the questioning eyes.

"Now I expect if freedom does come that some of you will pack up your bags and head off down that old dirt road over there to see where your lives lead you. I couldn't really blame any of you for that. I also expect some of you who have been with me a longer time will want to stay here and try to earn a living. For the ones who think they may want to stay, I've got to warn you that if the Southern states break away from the North, we will probably have a war. There could be huge armies marching through the countryside, trying to convince all the folks that their way is the right way to do things. Lots of people will probably get killed. I know plenty of Southern boys who are riled up about this issue with the Yanks. I'm also afraid that many farms will be destroyed. Let's just pray we are spared."

Jeremiah paused to light his pipe. Everyone watched the match flare up and the flame draw in to the pipe as the old man inhaled deeply.

"For you and me, it will probably mean that the markets where we sell our tobacco, cotton, and vegetables will dry up. If there is nowhere to sell what we grow, then there won't be money for any of us. If this happens, then we will all be on our own to survive however we can. I pray to God every day that there will be something I can do to make all of this go away and that we can keep living our lives like we always have. What's happening, though, is much bigger than any of us. I've spoken my piece to the politicians, and they all want blood. Something is going to happen, and I'm afraid it will be bad. I promise you, though, that every time I get some news I will let you know about it. That is all I can promise any of you at this point."

Old Joseph stepped forward again.

"Masr Yopp, all this talk about not havin' no money don't mean nothin' to us 'cause we ain't never had none no way. I think I seen a quarter last year and ain't a dime been in my pocket this year. All we is interested in is havin' a place to sleep, a place to raise our babies, and some greens and a few rabbits on the tables. If'n you can't sell the corn, then let's jes use it ourselves to stay alive until this dark cloud passes over, 'til them crazy Yankees get their heads straight or get whupped by our boys. If'n you can't sell the tobaccy or cotton, then let's grow onions or taters in them fields, something we can eat."

Several slaves nodded in agreement, and Yopp could hear voices backing up what Joseph had said.

"That sounds reasonable," Yopp replied. He rubbed his hands across his tired eyes.

"I hope it will be that simple, Joseph. Let's all pray to the Lord tonight and every night that we can keep our farm, our homes, and our families right here at Whitehall."

—

Following Jeremiah's speech, the slaves grew quiet as they all considered what may lay ahead. There was so much fear and uncertainty in the air that night that it had been suffocating. Each person's head was filled with questions, but there weren't any answers. Their worries soon turned to prayers. Some prayed that their homes and families would be protected, and some prayed for freedom and escaping to the North. Bill's father later told him that he couldn't even guess which of the slaves were praying for freedom, but when the war started, he learned that all but a few of the younger men wanted to stay on the farm.

Over the next year, Jeremiah met with the slaves several times and told them the latest news regarding the possible war. A sense of underlying fear permeated the plantation as everyone tried to continue their lives in a normal fashion.

This continued for almost two years until Jeremiah called another meeting with the slaves one night in 1861 to tell them the bad news. The war had started. Some hot headed boys in Charleston had shot up the Union fort and declared war.

Bill recalled that the happiest years of their lives came crashing down like a dead tree in a wind storm, and the black clouds of war rolled in and shut out the light. They were all blind and could not see their future.

Bill Yopp would turn a skinny sixteen years old that year as the South prepared for war.

GO CHASE YOUR DREAMS BEFORE THEY SLIP AWAY

APRIL 1861

Bill recalled that he ran so fast back to the big house after Jeremiah told the slaves the war had begun that he was waiting on the front steps when Jeremiah and Thomas arrived. He was out of breath and trembling with fear, wanting to find out what Thomas thought of all this madness. Until that time, Bill had not sensed that the talk of war would truly affect him. Thomas put his hand on Bill's shoulder and asked the teenager to sit down in one of the rocking chairs on the front porch. Bill knew this was serious because he had never been allowed to sit in these chairs.

No sooner had Bill taken a seat than Thomas poured him his first glass of brandy from a crystal decanter that sat on a nearby table. Bill was mesmerized by the crystal goblet, which had always been off limits to his hands. He held the delicate glass up and studied how the light from the porch lantern danced through it like sunny reflections on a mirrored brook. Thomas raised his glass in a toast to the war, took a drink, and told Bill to go ahead and do the same.

Young Bill slowly brought the glass to his lips and took a nervous swallow. The brandy had no sooner touched his throat than his eyes grew as large as hen's eggs. A look of distress and pain quickly spread across his dark face. He opened his mouth, letting out a long exhale that made a dreadful sound as if he had just swallowed a cup full of molten lead. The boy's eyes darted about, frantically searching for anything that would extinguish the roaring brush fire in his throat. His only solution was the horse-watering trough in front of the porch. Without a second thought, he raced to the trough and dunked his head into the water, up to his shoulders. Thomas laughed so loudly that almost everyone in the house came outside to see what was happening. Thomas later told Bill that he sounded like an old boar hog sloshing his face in a bucket of slop.

Bill later said that after his mouth cooled off and the excitement died down, Thomas told him that he was going to join up with the Confederate Army to go fight the Yankees. He said there had been lots of talk about a company of men from the county forming up in the summer and that he had already been talking with several of the officers that would lead it. They wanted him to be a lieutenant.

Bill sat there in the big rocking chair with his burning mouth, the water from the trough running off of his head, and the tears welling up in his eyes. He had never felt hurt in his heart like he felt right then, when he realized his best friend was leaving for war. Bill knew that when Thomas left, they wouldn't be seeing each other again for a long time. He couldn't imagine what it would be like around there with him gone. Nobody to hunt and fish with, nobody to tell jokes to. It would be awful.

Thomas understood the pain Bill was feeling. He walked over to Bill, put his hand on his shoulder, and tried to reassure and console him. He had heard talk that they could probably whip the Yankees in less than two years and that those years would go by lots faster than they could even imagine.

Thomas leaned forward. "Bill, you and I have had many a good time together over the years, and I intend for us to have our share in the future. We'll just look on this war like a short delay. That's all it is."

Bill tried to be strong. He fought back the tears as best he could. Thomas kept talking, saying things to try to make Bill feel better. However, his words were all like water off a duck's back. None of it stuck, and Bill didn't hear a word of it. He was busy thinking of his own plan.

The conversation grew silent. The only sounds that could be heard were the lonely call of a whip–poor–will off in the woods and some faraway laughter from the children inside the house. Bill walked over to where Thomas was sitting on the steps and stood in front of him.

He wiped the tears out of his eyes with the backs of his hands and said, "Masr, if you ain't goin' to stay here, then there ain't but one way to solve this problem. I reckon I gots to go with you. After all, you goin' to need Bill even more in the army than you do around here."

Thomas' face grew serious with concentration and surprise. He didn't quite know what to say when Bill made the offer. He mumbled a few words, then said, "Bill, the Confederate Army does not allow colored folks to be fighting men in the army. I think I heard that they would let coloreds be musicians, like a fife player or a drummer or something like that. Also, there's some talk about drafting a company of slaves to go along to take care of our camps and dig trenches, work like that. If you were allowed to go, I can't guarantee that you wouldn't get into some of that kind of hard work."

"That's fine by me as long as I'm with you," Bill answered. "I been playin' a cane flute since I was a baby, and I know I can beat on a drum. Don't take no book learning to do either one. I can handle a shovel as good as any old field slave, and ain't nobody goin' to beat Bill when it comes to cookin'. I learned almost everything my mama knows about that. I jes want us to be together." Thomas looked down at the old Blue Tick hound asleep at his feet and thought about everything that Bill had said.

"Well, I'll tell you what, Bill. You go talk with your mammy and pappy. Tell them what you want to do, and if they say it's all right with them, I'll talk with the colonel and see what he can do. I can't make any promises to you, though."

Bill eyes got as big as silver dollars with excitement.

"Oh, thank you, Masr. Thank you," Bill said as he grabbed Thomas' right hand and started shaking it. Bill was smiling so much that his face looked as if it was going to split like a ripe melon. "I'll go talk with my folks right now."

—

Bill raced off to the kitchen. He found his mother cleaning up a few things before her long workday ended. She flashed him one of her big smiles when he ran into the room.

"Mama," he called out, "I needs to talk with you and Daddy about what me and the Masr's going to do."

About that time, William walked in the back door with a load of firewood. He dropped it in the big box next to the fireplace.

"William, your boy says he has something important that he wants to talk with you and me about," Lia said as she dried the last pot and hung it on a peg on the wall. "Let's sit down over here next to the fire and hear him out. My feet are hurtin' so bad from standin' all day that I need to sit and rub on them."

Within seconds, William and Lia were seated on a bench while Bill stood. The boy was so fidgety and had so much nervous energy that his mother became irritated.

"Bill, sit yourself down and talk straight to us, young un'. I can't listen to no jumpin' jack. And how did you get so wet all over? You goin' to catch your death of cold, boy."

Bill quickly sat down in a chair across from his father and looked down at the flickering fire.

"Oh, it's a long story. I'll tell you later," the boy said nervously as he looked up into his mother's eyes.

"What's you got in your head tonight?" Bill's father asked.

"Well, I was talking with Masr Thomas a few minutes ago, and he told me that he plans to join up as a lieutenant with the Confederate Army in Dublin this summer. He said it was jes fine if I went with him. He said I would have to be a drummer or some kind of flute player or a cook and that I wouldn't be in no fightin'. I did some serious thinkin' about this, and it's something I truly want to do."

William and Lia both felt a rush of fear, dread, and panic race through their bodies, quite unlike anything either of them had experienced before. The last time William had felt a shock like that was when he nearly stepped on a Timber Rattler down in the cypress swamp.

Their immediate reaction was to look at each other with searching eyes in hope that one of them would step forward with a quick response to their son's request.

William leaned forward and spoke first.

"Let me make sure we understand this. You wants to go off to war with Masr Thomas? And you wants to fight against them Yankee boys who says they want to free us slaves? I must have some cotton lint in my ears or somethin'. Did I hear you right?" he said. He put his right forefinger in one of his ears in an obvious effort to act out his confusion.

Bill squirmed in his chair but looked his parents squarely in the eyes. At that moment both of Bill's parents reached the same conclusion: Bill was no longer simply a boy, but a young man who was ready to live his life as he saw fit.

"Yes, suh," Bill replied as he sat erect in the chair. "You know that Masr Thomas and me are kind of like brothers. I can't remember but a few days in my whole life that he and I weren't together. He's going to be a big officer and will need me to help him with his cookin' and keepin' his horse fed and groomed. There's lots I can do for him. He said that it was just fine with him if I went as long as I got your blessings."

There was another long, uncomfortable pause. Before his parents could say anything, he spoke up again.

"Y'all have got to understand that I don't see this as fighting to keep slavery. You know how I feel about that. My decision don't have nothing to do with anything except friendship. The Masr wouldn't have said it was all right for me to go unless he really wanted me to be with him, too. And the Masr thinks that the Rebs will lick those Yankees in no time at all. Before you know it, we'll all be right back here like nothing ever happened."

William took a deep breath. Worry was etched all over his brown satin face when he stood up and walked slowly over to the fire to poke the coals. Bill could see a faraway, terrified look in his father's eyes as he stood there nervously moving the coals around with the long iron poker. Lia's eyes also glanced from Bill's anxious face to the hypnotic flames of the fire. Bill noticed that her eyes shifted from the fire to William's eyes in an effort to read his mind.

William broke the silence again.

"Bill, you know there ain't nobody I respect more than Masr Jeremiah and Masr Thomas. I truly understand about your friendship with Thomas. When you was borned the preacher read us a verse about children being a gift from God, and that is the way we have always felt. You have been one of the best gifts anyone could ever give us. If we ever had to choose between you or our freedom, we would choose you every time. The good Lawd tells each of us to walk in love, setting aside our desires, denying our self–will, and grabbin' hold of the high calling of being a parent. It's our job to take care of you and keep you safe. If you go off to war then we can't do that. We can't be there to protect you the way the Lawd asked us to."

"Daddy," Bill replied anxiously, "You and Mama know that every time somebody reads the Bible to us, I do my best to remember every word. I know that y'all have worked hard to raise all of us children with good hearts and smart heads. You have done more than your share of what the Lawd asked you to do. Now it's time for me to do what the Lawd has asked me to do. There is one verse from the Bible that I know is talking about me and Thomas. It's the one from Proverbs that you and Mama have been preaching to me since I was a little baby. It says, 'A man of many companions may come to ruin, but there is a friend who sticks closer than a brother.' I ain't got but one really good friend and that is Thomas. I can't turn my back on him now when he needs me more than ever."

Tears filled Lia's eyes and streamed down her cheeks. She knew that Bill was right, and she had no strong argument to change his mind. Loyalty and friendship were difficult adversaries for a mother's love. She could only pray to God that he would keep her son safe and bring him home soon. She got up from the bench, walked over to Bill, pulled his head close to her heart, and kissed his forehead.

As Bill sat in the chair, Lia caressed his smooth face with her hands and looked deeply into his dark eyes.

"I kissed this forehead right in this room sixteen years ago when you were first born," she said. "That's a lot of years, and you've been a mighty fine boy." She wiped her cheeks with her apron. "You are a man now and I know that I gots to let you go. You and Masr Thomas go chase your dreams before they slip away. Go with God and come home safe and sound. Your old Mama will be waitin' right here to hug your neck and take care of you when you come back."

THEY STOOD IN LINE FOR SLOOSH

JULY, 1861

The summer was a dizzying swirl of heat, tears, long days, and anticipation for Bill Yopp and the 1,100 young men of the 14th Georgia Volunteer Infantry Regiment. The unit, comprised of ten companies of men from ten surrounding counties, was scheduled to depart in mid July, so the new troopers busied themselves with those things that men preparing to go to war do. They hastily completed what farming or business chores they could. They made sure their sons, brothers, parents, and wives knew everything that needed to be done during their absence. They had long, melancholy talks with their wives and sweethearts about the importance of the war and the sadness they would carry in their hearts. The lawyers burned the midnight oil as men lined up to prepare their wills and other legal papers in case they did not make the journey home. Mothers and wives made new uniforms and socks. Fathers cleaned up old guns for their sons and made sure they knew how to shoot them. And some men drank whiskey, celebrating the upcoming adventure until the wee hours of the morning. It was as if they hoped the whiskey would make the adventure seem more heroic than it already was.

Bill had been so excited about his upcoming journey

that he was not even aware of the human emotion called 'homesickness' until the evening before the regiment was to leave. Bill had never been away from home.

As the last rays of sunlight turned the color of a ripe peach over the western fields at Whitehall, everyone on the plantation made their way up to the big house. The stately columned home always looked magical at twilight when the oil lanterns were lit and the warmth of the home reflected the evening sunset colors. The slaves came to wish Bill and the young master a safe journey and offered their prayers that they would return soon. As he and Thomas stood on the big front porch proudly showing off their newly made Confederate uniforms, Bill felt a knot of peculiar emotion and a longing for the comforts of home, even though he had not yet left. It was a strange and troubling sentiment that he had never before experienced. Not until his mother sat on the edge of his bed that night and kissed his cheek did he fully appreciate what his home and family meant to him. As she pulled away, several warm tears splashed on his face, letting him know that she felt even more strongly about him leaving than he did. Flashing thoughts of remaining at Whitehall were dulled by the stark realization that he had officially enlisted and could not back out of his responsibility.

It was a long night filled with apprehension, expectancy, and concern. Before he knew it, the raspberry sun had inched over the moss–draped treetops and colored the windows with those warm and comfortable morning shadows that forever dance through the memories of home.

After boisterous celebrations and teary farewells in Dublin, Company H, also known as The Blackshear Guards, marched northwest toward Macon on July 9. Bill led them, proudly beating his new drum. He hadn't learned how to play it yet, but that would come during their basic training. Thomas had told him to play anything that helped the men march in proper cadence. Bill looked more like a grown man than a sixteen–year–old in his new homespun gray uniform and forage cap. His mother had lovingly packed him a satchel of biscuits, cookies, and other treats that he had slung around his shoulder. From a distance, he could faintly hear her final motherly words.

"Now don't you forget to eat plenty of greens and vegetables, and keep your feet warm and dry in the winter. You get back here to see us as soon as you can."

Shortly after leaving Dublin, Thomas was promoted from first lieutenant to captain and was given the responsibility of being the company commander. He rode on a big black stallion in front of "H" company, which was comprised of 130 of Laurens County's finest young men. Everything felt completely normal with Bill marching beside Thomas. Hardly five minutes passed that they didn't look at each other and smile.

The adventure had begun.

—

The march to Macon took four days. By the time they arrived, most of the men were sporting new blisters on their feet from wearing the ill–fitting boots or shoes they had been given. Many of the farm boys who had never owned a pair of shoes or boots had removed them before they were halfway to Macon. None of the fresh faced boys realized that before the war was over they would march hundreds upon hundreds of miles and their feet would become as tough as a strap of leather. The reality of the glamorous escapade was just beginning to sink in.

Upon arriving in Macon, the troops were crowded into dozens of boxcars like salt herring in a barrel. Others sat on the sides of long open flatcars that were stacked high with supplies. Realizing the discomfort inside the cramped and stuffy boxcars and knowing that Bill had never ridden on a train, Thomas made certain that they got prime seats on the roof of a boxcar.

Years later Thomas often laughed about the smile that came across Bill's face as they climbed atop the box-car and how "Bill was grinning like a cat that had just eaten a canary the full ninety miles to Atlanta." Their only dilemma came when the wind shifted and blew the smoke and cinders from the wood–fired steam engine back along the top of the train, covering their new uniforms in soot. A white soldier sitting next to Bill gagged on the smoke and complained, "Will ya look at me? I'm all black now, just like you!"

Bill leaned over, shook the man's hand briskly, and replied, "Welcome to the family."

Everyone on the rooftop howled at Bill's joke.

—

A few miles south of Atlanta, the long train slowly squealed to a stop near the largest encampment of men and supplies that any of these soldiers had ever seen. As far as they could see in every direction, thousands of troopers were marching in formations, taking bayonet instructions, shooting on rifle ranges, and sitting in groups as officers lectured them. In the distance, Bill saw a battery of cannons fire from one hill to another as the artillerymen practiced their new trade. Small white tents and smoky campfires dotted the red clay landscape on every knoll and down in every valley. Bill chuckled because the thousands of men swarming through the camp looked like ants around a spilled jar of molasses.

The new troopers grew quiet and somber as they gazed out over the mass of humanity and suddenly realized the war was real. This would be their home for at least two weeks of basic training. After that they would receive their first real military assignment.

As the green troops poured into the makeshift training camp, the excitement and enthusiasm climbed to a fever pitch. The men were anxious to find the Yankees and show them a thing or two about Southern hospitality. The Blackshear Guards marched proudly down a tent–lined dusty road to their bivouac area. Every so often a soldier on the sidelines would yell out asking where they were from and call out their own home county.

"You boys ready to shoot some blue bellies?" The call came from a group standing around one of the few shade trees in camp.

A soldier right behind Bill hollered back that all the Yanks had high–tailed it north when they heard The Blackshear Guards were coming to town. Everyone laughed. They felt a surge of pride each time they heard the name of their unit called out. Captain Yopp felt especially good when he sensed for the first time that the men were becoming a team.

Not long after arriving at the big training camp, the men were herded through the supply depot, where they were issued their personal gear. It consisted of a cartridge box, cap box, belt, bayonet and scabbard, haversack, two tin pans, a canteen, a bucket to use for cooking, an Enfield rifle and ammunition, and three breadths of osnaburgs, bolts of cloth–like canvas used for their tents. Each man carried half of a tent that he could quickly assemble. Company H was lucky because they received all of their required supplies. The Confederate units who joined the fray later in 1861 and during the remainder of the war were issued very few personal items and were forced to rely exclusively on gathering these things from fallen comrades or the enemy on the battlefield. Since Negroes were not allowed to fight, Bill was given only the basic camp gear and none of the weaponry. That was just fine with him since the thought of shooting at anything other than a possum or coon had no appeal for him.

Bill had assumed that his summer working in the

tobacco barns was the worst heat he would ever experience, but late July in Atlanta at a dusty army training encampment took the prize. By ten o'clock each morning, the camp was a filthy, shimmering pocket of one hundred degree heat. He heard one boy say that it was so hot he had seen a bird using a potholder to pull a worm out of the ground. Another soldier who was trying to outdo his friend yelled, "It's so hot down here that we're eatin' peppers just to cool our mouths down."

The stifling heat and humidity was almost unbearable, especially to the boys who were not accustomed to working in it. Hardly an hour went by that Bill didn't see some poor soul collapse from the heat and taken to the field hospital. He heard that two boys from another regiment had died from the heat and it didn't take Captain Yopp long to pull the company together to warn them about the danger. Bill spent many an hour hauling water buckets to the trainees before the heat wave broke and the temperatures dropped from around one hundred to a cool eighty–five degrees.

The drummers were assigned to work daily with the regimental drum major. He taught the boys how to manipulate the sticks and play the various beats. Bill quickly learned that the drummers and fife players did not have an easy life in the army. They were the first to arise each morning at 5:45, when the lead drummer sounded the Drummer's Call. This call assembled all of the musicians and alerted the troops to get ready. Once all of the drummers were assembled, they would beat out the second call for formation in unison. During camp, the musician's day was filled with no less than a dozen other calls for everything from the Surgeon's Call telling the sick to go to the infirmary to special drill calls. Their day ended at 10:30 p.m. when Taps was played, signaling everyone to extinguish all lights.

At the end of each day when Bill removed the drum strap from around his neck, he was completely exhausted. The combination of the heat and the weight of the drum was almost unbearable, but he could feel himself getting stronger with each passing day. He frequently found himself trying to help the younger drummers, some as young as twelve years old, who often cried because they could no longer carry their heavy drum. Their vision of an exciting, fun-filled life in the army was not living up to their youthful expectations. Many were sent home during those first weeks. Bill constantly worried that the children would collapse on long marches and be left behind. He tried to offer encouragement and assistance to them whenever possible. If he saw one wavering in the heat, he would make sure that Thomas or another officer knew about it so someone would take care of the boy.

After less than a week in the training camp, Bill's day had already begun to take on a well-ordered schedule. His reputation as an excellent cook quickly spread among the officers of the regiment, and, as a result, he frequently found himself preparing elaborate meals for Captain Yopp and his friends. Following his early morning drummer duties, his days started with cooking breakfast for the officers. His specialty was a dish called "sloosh," which consisted of cornmeal wrapped around the end of a rifle ramrod. It was then "slooshed" in bacon grease and held over an open flame until it was crisp. The smell of those bacon flavored corn muffins drifting through the camp each morning brought many a man to stand in line for his sloosh.

When breakfast was completed, Bill would start brushing and cleaning Thomas' uniform, shining his gear, cleaning guns, or grooming his horse. He also found himself cleaning the officer's living quarters, washing clothes, and foraging through the camp and countryside for supplies. When all of that work was finished, he would race off to train with the drummers. It was a back breaking schedule, but Bill enjoyed every minute of it.

Bill's reputation as a conscientious worker also spread quickly among the enlisted men of Company H. Almost daily someone new would approach him and ask for his assistance with some chore, which he seldom turned down. All he asked in return for his work, regardless of the job, was a payment of ten cents, which the men gladly gave him. Thus the nickname "Ten Cent Bill," or "Ten" for short, took hold and stuck. A home cooked meal or a well–polished pair of boots was worth much more than a dime to a soldier who still had a pocket full of dollars that his father or mother gave him when he left home. On any given evening, it was not uncommon to hear someone call out, "Ten, how about cookin' some of those tasty beans for me?" The reply was always the same. "Yes, suh. Come see me in thirty minutes, and bring your dime."

Bill and Thomas soon learned that one of their favorite times of the day was late in the evening after all the work was done. They would sit beside the campfire talking about their day's work and what was scheduled for the next day. They also shared any news from home that may have come from new troops joining the unit. Thomas would tell Bill about any war news he had picked up from regimental headquarters. The bond of friendship and respect between Bill and Thomas grew even stronger as they both relied upon the talents of the other for survival in their new life. Thomas often told Bill how proud he was of the excellent job Bill did in the camp and that the other men constantly bragged about his abilities and pleasant attitude. Bill passed similar compliments along to Thomas, telling him how much the soldiers in the company respected him as their leader. Thomas also relied upon Bill to let him know of any problems the enlisted men were having that perhaps they were not willing to share with an officer.

As the hot summer days rolled by, it became obvious to Bill that Negro body servants were not an oddity in the army camp. Large numbers of slaves accompanied both officers and enlisted men from slaveholding families when they marched off to war. Bill quickly learned that most slaves considered it a great honor to be selected to accompany their masters into battle, the same sentiment he had.

The life of a body servant in the Confederate camps during the early stages of war was generally not strenuous. Their responsibilities were all similar to what Bill was experiencing. The servants of cavalrymen were required to help with the horses, and the servants of artillerymen helped clean and move the cannons. There was nothing complicated about the system.

When a soldier was a member of a mess, usually four to six men who cooked and ate together, the servant would do the washing and cleaning for them all, and the other members of the mess would contribute to the slave's maintenance. Most servants enjoyed a great deal of freedom within the camps, which gave all of them the opportunity to earn money by doing odd jobs for other soldiers.

For the first time in Bill's life, he was being paid to perform a chore. On most farms, slaves were forbidden to even possess money. Since this was a completely new experience for him, it resulted in a burning enthusiasm to collect as many coins as possible. He learned quickly that money meant power, and he soon carried as much money in his haversack as some of the officers. Very few nights went by when he did not spread out his money on his blanket and examine every coin by the light of a coal oil lantern, imagining what shiny things he could buy with them. He wished constantly that his mama and daddy could see his money because he was the first member of their family that had ever earned any. They would be very proud of him.

It didn't take the high–ranking Confederate officers long to realize that their system of military slave labor added tremendously to the strength of the army. By having slaves who would do all of the menial chores within the camps plus the strenuous work of digging trenches and building forts, the white soldiers were freed up to focus on the primary matter at hand: fighting the Yankees and winning. As long as the slaves were willing participants, it made for a winning combination during the early years of the war. It was a definite advantage that the Union forces did not have.

As the short but grueling training period came to a close, the men learned that they would soon be moving out to join with Robert E. Lee's Army of Northern Virginia.

———

"I ain't ever heard the likes of the yellin' that morning when the captain rode into camp and told us to pack up," Bill said to Sam. He smiled. "Within an hour there was thousands of men singin' and marchin', and I know that my drums had never sounded better. We were proud as peacocks during our five–mile march to the big train depot in Atlanta where the boxcars were waiting for us. I'll never forget the thousands of folks that lined the dusty roads to wish us well. Pretty young ladies ran out and hugged and kissed the boys. Others ran into the road and gave us bread or candy and cookies. Little boys chased along beside our company and pretended to be marching with us. I recall this one lady that came up to Captain Yopp and said, 'Sir, my son is an officer with General Lee in Virginia. Please accept this food from me and pray that some other mother is offering food and hospitality to my son today, wherever he is.' The Captain graciously accepted the cookies and tipped his hat in appreciation."

It took the regiment almost a full day to load all its men and equipment on the trains that were headed north to Lynchburg, Virginia. If all went well, the four hundred mile trip would take about fourteen hours. The heat wave showed no signs of letting up, but the men had been promised that the Virginia mountains would be like a cool springtime day. Only two boys in Company H had ever seen a real mountain, so their descriptions of the new geography were mesmerizing and exciting to the others. "You mean that the ground jes shoots straight up for as far as you can see?" Bill had asked one of the boys.

"Yep, it's like God reached down from heaven, grabbed a fist full of rocks and trees, and yanked them straight away into the sky. Some of them is so high that you can't even see the tops fer the clouds."

"We chattered like a bunch of children, partly because we was just plain nervous and partly because deep down inside we were sure that this big adventure would soon take a turn for the worse."

DEATH BECAME THEIR PAINFUL COMPANION

AUGUST, 1861

The monotonous drone of the clattering rails put some of the weary soldiers to sleep soon after their departure from Atlanta. Most of the boys never relaxed, though. Each time they felt their eyes getting heavy, they would round another bend in the track, and there, staring them in the face, would be a stunning new vista like nothing they had ever seen. The expansive cotton and cornfields of Georgia gradually gave way to rocky outcroppings with rushing whitewater streams and rivers. The choking heat and dust of Atlanta transformed into the cool clear air that floated through the mountains and foothills and invigorated the body and soul. The tall Georgia pines and oaks were replaced by fir, cedar, and ash trees that grew from cracks in the sheer granite outcroppings, which, according to most of these boys, was the "darndest thing [they] ever seen."

"We can't even get tobaccy to grow in the dirt in our county, and they can get fifty foot trees to grow out of rocks up here. Probably a good place to farm," one boy said to another quite seriously. "That is, if you could keep from fallin' off the mountain while you were plowin'."

During the train ride Bill sat beside a skinny mop–headed corporal named Josiah Bellflower. He was a thirty–two–year–old school teacher from Dublin. Bill and Josiah had struck up a friendship during the past week when Bill had performed several chores for him. As it turned out, the mess that Josiah belonged to was exceedingly deficient in having anyone who could cook a meal that was fit for human consumption. Josiah told Bill that their cook was so bad that he thought he had to flip a pot of water over to get it to boil on both sides. Bill took his word for it and prayed he wouldn't get an invite to dinner.

With starvation as a backdrop, Josiah made an arrangement with Bill that profoundly changed the drummer's life and probably saved Josiah's. The corporal offered thirty minutes of his time each night to teach Bill to read and write in exchange for one good meal per day. When Bill excitedly told Captain Yopp about Josiah's offer and asked for his permission, the captain was elated. In fact, the captain pulled some strings at headquarters and located a small chalkboard, chalk, a box of pencils, and a stack of writing paper. He presented it as a surprise to Bill and Josiah shortly before their first teaching session. Both men were overjoyed with the supplies, and Bill promised that he would study hard and be a good student.

The night after his first writing lesson, Bill sat in his tent looking at his scribbling marks on a wrinkled piece of paper. Josiah said the letters represented his name. Bill felt so much pride that he thought his chest would explode. His goal was to write a letter to his parents by himself before Christmas.

—

The next four weeks were a blur rushing to a new location, setting up camp, and waiting for something to happen. No sooner had Bill's regiment arrived in Lynchburg, Virginia, than they were ordered to ship out across the mountains to West Virginia. There, the Yankees were making some faint efforts to take over key crossroads, bridges, or strategic mountaintops. The boys were itching for a fight, but it seemed like every time they moved to a new location the Yankees were either not around or there were so few that the skirmishes were small and short. As a result, the regiment would rush to a new location, dig in, and wait for days on end with no action.

There seemed to be no present danger in the war, yet the regiment continued to be shuffled around. They finally moved back into a mountainous area north of Lynchburg, where things settled into a boring routine of survival.

Soon the chilly autumn mornings in the Virginia mountains made the boys realize that the upcoming winter weather could be their biggest enemy. The men busied themselves with trying to make their living conditions more bearable. Then, as if God had decided to punish them for telling one too many foul jokes or for gambling or drinking, a series of fatal mishaps befell the 14th. It all began when they camped in a crowded valley and drank contaminated water from the only stream in the area.

By early October, over half of the 1,100 men in the regiment were so sick with dysentery that they could hardly march. By mid October, over forty men had died from the sickness, and another thirty–four had died when the measles swept through the weakened troops. Measles were bad enough for the boys who had no immunity to the disease; most died a slow miserable death from the raging fever it brought. Adding dysentery to the formula meant higher fevers, infection, diarrhea, vomiting, and the most miserable death imaginable.

As if the outbreaks of measles and dysentery were not enough, it seemed as though it rained the entire month of October. Bill knew that it did not let up for eleven straight days and resulted in the most wretched living conditions anyone could imagine. The temperatures at night dropped to near freezing, and the camp became a sticky mire that would have made any pig feel right at home.

Low cold clouds hung tight over their heads almost every day and made them shiver to the bone. The sun was nonexistent, and none of the men had a dry thread of clothing. Anything made out of cotton began to rot, and soon the soldiers looked like a group of castaways who had been lost on a desert island. According to some statisticians, the sickness and storms of that fateful October in Virginia would cost the 14th regiment more men, sick and dead, than the battle of Manassas Plains without a single shot being fired. Bill was not spared from sickness. He lost over fifteen pounds from dysentery before he was able to recuperate to a point where he could perform his duties again. His many friends, including Thomas, nursed him back to health. Once he had regained his strength,

Bill spent most of his waking hours taking care of his sick friends and trying to make them more comfortable. Death marched through their camps daily and quickly became a painful companion for the men of the 14th.

—

"Masr Thomas," Bill began in a weak and shaky voice as he stood in the doorway to the large tent. "I needs to go home for a while to see my folks and get well. I am home-sick and body sick something awful. I'm afraid that if I stay around this here death camp much longer, you'll be a plantin' me in one of them boxes with the other dead boys. Can you and me go to Whitehall for a few weeks?" he pleaded with Thomas as he stood and wrung his hands.

The request caught Thomas off guard. He had been so engrossed in trying to get his company back on its feet that he had not even thought about home. He had spent countless hours working with the doctors and medical staff doing whatever could be done to give his sick men some comfort. One of the most difficult things he had had to do was educate the men to boil all of their drinking water, which was virtually impossible in the wet conditions. He had also been working long hours at headquarters trying to convince the higher ranking officers that Company H was in no shape to march into battle until the troops were over their illnesses and had regained their strength. In spite of his pleas, the regiment found themselves moving to a minor skirmish almost every two weeks.

Realizing that no man deserved a break from the

horrid life he was living more than Bill, Thomas quickly granted his request. He knew that the cost of train tickets and food for the long trip home would use most of Bill's hard–earned money, so he gave Bill ten dollars.

"Here you go, Bill," Thomas said as he put a gold coin in Bill's hand. "Use this money to buy yourself a train ticket and some food. If you get home and decide to stay there, I'll be fine with that. Just send me a letter and let me know what you are doing. Wish I could go with you, but I can't."

Bill stood in Thomas' tent looking at the shiny gold coin, the first such coin he had ever held.

"I can't take your money, Masr. I got money I can spend." He held the coin out to return it to Thomas.

Thomas sat down in the small chair next to the table in his tent and struck a match to light his pipe. He took a deep draw and exhaled the wispy smoke into the chilly, dimly lit tent. In the dancing candle shadows, Bill noticed hints of white appearing in Thomas' dark hair. The war was taking its toll in small ways on enlisted men and officers alike.

"I know you have some money, Bill," he said. "But you worked hard for every penny of that, and I think you ought to buy some nice things for your family with it."

Bill was very nearly overwhelmed with emotion, partly from the realization that he would be going home and partly because of the generosity of his friend. He looked down at the ground and then brought his hands to his eyes as several tears ran down his cheeks.

"You are the best Masr that any slave ever had. I don't see no way that I will ever be able to make it up to you, but I sho' will try."

"And Bill," Thomas said as he stood up from the short stool, "I don't want you calling me Master ever again. I see us as equals in this war. From now on you call me Captain Yopp in public and Thomas in private."

Bill was stunned and didn't quite know what to say. He could call his master by his first name. This was unheard of. It would be difficult for him to break old habits, but this small sign of equality swelled in his chest like the heart of a young lover on his sweetheart's doorstep.

"That's mighty kind of you, Masr. Uh, Captain Thomas." Bill smiled and chuckled. "Now you gots me all confused."

—

Thomas and Bill talked late into the night about Bill's trip. Thomas wrote out an official pass and told Bill that he should protect it with his life. If he was caught without it, he could be in deep trouble. He also told Bill how to go about getting to the train station, buying his ticket, transferring trains in Atlanta, and finally getting himself back to Whitehall. It was all quite intimidating to Bill, but he was determined to be self–sufficient and find his way home. The plan was for him to leave in two days and ride with the supply wagons back to Lynchburg. He would simply retrace his steps home from there.

Before Bill went to sleep the next night, he made the

rounds to all of the boys from Company H, telling them that he was going to Dublin in case they wanted to send letters home. He also walked through the mud the two miles down to the field hospital to make the same offer to the boys who were sick. He said he would deliver the letters to the post office when he got home. As a result of Bill's offer, the camp was unusually quiet that night as men dictated letters to the few soldiers who could write.

While Bill sat in his tent, he could plainly hear Private Patterson in the next tent dictating a heartrending letter to Josiah Bellflower, who hastily wrote over a dozen letters that night for his friends.

My darling Lou,

Life has been miserable up here since the rains started. It's almost impossible to keep dry. Some days I stay in my dripping tent and just think about you and the children, wishing for the warmth of our house and your sweet embrace. I think of you every day and wish I could be there to walk down the lane at sunset with you, see you smile, and hear you laugh. I miss the kids something awful and wish I could be there to help you with the farm. We haven't had much fighting, but lots of boys are getting sick and dying from some stomach sickness and the measles. I was standing next to Ezekial Johnson's bed in the hospital when he went to his reward last week. I sure was sad about that since we were good friends. Be sure to tell Lucy that Ezekial spoke her name at the very end and said he loved her. I have been lucky and haven't gotten sick. If this rain would stop, I'd be happier. It's mighty hard even getting a fire to start at night. Write me soon and let me know how everything is going for you and the children.

Your devoted husband,
James Patterson

Captain Yopp wrote up a list of all of the sickly soldiers and a summary of what action they had seen. He was having Bill post it in Dublin since no newspaper was operating there during the war. He also wrote personal letters to the wives and parents of the dead soldiers to tell them how brave their husbands or sons had been before they died.

Shortly before Taps was blown at 10:30 p.m., dozens of somber soldiers lined up at Bill's tent. Each person had one or more letters and a quiet, pleading request that Bill try to bring letters back to them from their families. They all offered Bill his standard fee of ten cents for payment, but he rejected every offer. He was doing this out of love for the men of Company H. As each man stepped forward, Bill felt more and more guilty that he was the one leaving and not them.

The rain let up around eight o'clock the next morning as Bill stood outside Captain Yopp's tent in his uniform, his haversack on his back. The mud and muck rose halfway up his boots and made a sucking sound as he walked. Several of Bill's good friends gathered around to wish him a safe journey.

"Cap'n," Bill said as he looked Thomas in the eyes, "I sho hate to leave you like this. I'll tell your mama and everyone how good you are doing and that you plan to be there for Christmas if all goes well."

"Have a safe trip, Bill," Thomas said. He gripped Bill's right hand and gave him a firm shake. "We'll miss you."

Bill could see that Thomas almost reached out to embrace him but pulled back when he saw the other men watching. As an officer, he could not show affection toward a soldier and Bill realized this. A moment of sadness rushed through Bill because he too wanted to give Thomas a hug and wish him well, but he knew he couldn't do that.

Bill jumped onto the front seat of the freight wagon as the driver leaned forward, snapping his long whip over the heads of the eight large mules. No sooner had Bill thrown his bag to the floor than the rain began pelting the soggy ground once again. The last view he had of the men of Company H was over his right shoulder as the wagon rounded a curve. Ten or twelve men were standing in ankle deep mud in the pouring rain, wishing that they could be leaving too. All the tears of homesickness that were shed that morning were perfectly camouflaged by the rain. Even Thomas found himself a little choked up as he watched the wagon disappear down the long muddy road, not knowing if he would ever see his friend again.

DELIVERING A STACK OF SORROWFUL LETTERS

NOVEMBER, 1861

Eight days and five hundred anxious miles later, Bill found himself jumping from the crowded train in Laurens County with a sense of excitement and expectation reminiscent of Christmas mornings in his master's house. Even though Bill had only been in the town of Dublin a few times, he knew this was home. After taking a few steps away from the busy train, he bent over and scooped up a handful of the powdery dark dirt. He felt its smoothness between his fingers and smiled. The sun was shining and his rain–drenched body was finally dry and warm. He stopped in a sunny spot in the street and found himself turning his face upwards to absorb the warmth and comfort of the sun that had been a stranger to him for weeks. Most of the onlookers thought he was odd to begin with, being a black boy in a Rebel uniform. His sun worship in the middle of the busy street convinced them that he had lost his mind.

Then it hit him like a painful shot through the heart. The exhilaration of being home was quickly tempered with the realization that he had to deliver the stack of sorrowful letters to the post office. He patted the bundle of letters in his sack, took a deep breath, and headed down the busy street. More than one head turned to look at him, and he just tipped his hat and wished them well. He went directly to the post office to deliver the dozens of letters given to him by the men of Company H.

The Confederate Postal Service had assumed control of the post office. It still functioned well within the Southern states, but the loss of most of the federal mail and budget cuts reduced manpower and the overall ability to post mail to anywhere outside of the Confederate states. The president of the Confederacy, Jefferson Davis, had ordered all local postmasters to make the delivery of letters to and from the troops a priority, especially when they knew the letters bore the sad news of death or injury. The postmasters had been ordered to drop whatever they were doing to make special deliveries to these families. Whenever a uniformed soldier walked into the post office, the workers held their breath in anticipation of bad news. No place witnessed sadness on a more regular basis than the wartime post office.

Most of the letters Bill delivered were letters of love and general news from the blockhouses and trenches. However, eight letters bore news of death. He was careful when he removed Captain Yopp's eight letters from the protective oilcloth because he knew their heartbreaking content. The few other customers in the small store quickly understood the importance of Bill's visit and stepped aside to allow him to move to the counter. Bill slowly unwrapped the cloth and realized he had never heard such silence or seen such solemn anticipation.

The customers edged closer to the postal counter

in an effort to see the addresses on the letters. A few people with loved ones in Company H shyly asked Bill what news he could share with them about their sons, husbands, or brothers. Luckily, these men were alive and healthy. Bill discovered it was a great pleasure telling them the happy news. He was terrified that if he stayed around long enough, though, one of the questions would focus on one of the eight dead men. He prayed he would not have to tell anyone the dreadful news.

The postmaster knew that many of the people receiving these letters could not read or write, so he and a few of his literate friends had to read the bad news to these families. It was an unwritten part of their job description. The old postmaster and his wife realized it would be a long day and night before he and a few grim–faced volunteers finished delivering the death notices to the far reaches of the county. A handful of conscientious citizens were on call for the postmaster to make the long wagon rides bringing news of death to unwitting relatives.

During the long train ride, Bill had held the package of letters in his hands and thought of the despair and suffering they would bring when they were read by some anxious parent or wife. In the time it would take to read the first paragraph of Captain Yopp's letter, their lives would be completely shattered. Wives would become widows, children would become fatherless, and parents would lose one of the most precious things in their lives. Quiet homes would be traumatized with screams of agony and suffering. Young children would be terrified because they wouldn't understand what was happening. Hope would disintegrate and leave families with a painful numbness like nothing they had felt before. Neighbors, nannies, and cooks would rush to hold and comfort the sobbing young children while their trembling mothers and grandparents cried in each other's arms, trying to console one another.

A fleeting thought had crossed Bill's mind. Perhaps if he conveniently lost the letters, the people could enjoy a few more weeks of happiness until the bad news reached them by some other means. In the end, though, he knew this was his responsibility. It was the high price he had to pay for his brief, warm, and delicious taste of home.

After completing his chores at the post office, Bill stepped back onto the street and immediately felt a sense of relief that this part of the journey was over. Unfortunately, though, he knew the worst part still lay ahead. While standing on the street he reached into his uniform jacket pocket and removed a letter that he had purposefully not given the postmaster. This letter had a big "X" marked on the top of it so he could recognize it as the letter Captain Yopp had written to Alice Pennington, the wife of Rafe Pennington. Rafe had been a neighbor and a good friend of Captain Yopp's. Bill knew him quite well from many fun days of hunting in the swamps and fields near Whitehall. Bill had promised Thomas that he would personally deliver the letter that told of Rafe's death. To make matters worse, since Alice could neither read nor write, Bill had agreed to tell her everything that Thomas wrote in the letter.

In spite of Bill's conscientious studies, he still had a long way to go before becoming proficient at reading and writing. So, prior to his departure from Virginia, Thomas had read the letter to Bill six times so that he could memorize his words. Bill's ability to quote the letter word for word had surprised Thomas, and it was one of the first times in Bill's life that he had attempted such a feat. It gave him great pleasure to be considered a "smart" man with an exceptional memory.

After receiving a warm meal at the back door of a boarding house, Bill set out to walk the eleven miles from Dublin to Rafe Pennington's farm. He had only traveled a few miles when he unexpectedly realized how quiet and serene this walk was compared to the marches he had led with the regiment. There was no drumming, no cloud of dust or ocean of mud, no clattering of pots and pans on the supply wagons, no horse or mule snorting, and no coughing or talking from the hundreds of soldiers behind him. Instead of distant cannon fire, he heard the rattling sound of a red headed woodpecker on a hollow sweet gum tree. Instead of the smell of rotting garbage, horse manure, and human waste, he smelled the crisp clean country air that was sweetly scented by tall yellow pines and honeysuckle. He stopped on the silent road and tasted the soothing serenity that only the quiet anticipation of coming home can serve.

On more than one occasion, he found himself turning around and looking back down the road to make certain that no troops were following him. He smiled when he realized how alone he was. He sang his favorite songs so loudly that he scattered a flock of redwing blackbirds from a nearby creek bottom that was thick with willow trees. He watched the birds rush into the sky as a single dark cloud, reading each other's minds in mid air as they twisted and darted in unison. Bill always enjoyed watching for the bright red patches on these bird's wings. He smiled when he thought of his mama's explanation that a drop of blood from Jesus on the cross had touched one's wing, causing these birds to forever have their distinctive markings.

He was still weak from the sickness he had endured in Virginia and found he had to stop and rest under a shady tree every hour or so. He noted to himself what a real pleasure it was to rest whenever he wanted.

He had walked about four miles when a gray bearded man driving a heavily loaded cotton wagon came up from behind and stopped beside him. The grizzled old man wore a floppy brown felt hat that almost hid his eyes. His belly stretched the few remaining buttons of his dirty shirt.

"Whar you goin' boy?" he said in a deep gravelly voice. "I'm heading down to Rafe Pennington's farm, suh," Bill replied as he removed his cap. He smiled.

The old man looked Bill over and then offered him a ride to keep him company. "I'm a headin' in that direction if you want to warm up this here seat next to me. I'll drop you off down at Rafe's place."

Bill gladly jumped up on the seat. He was immediately asked the question everyone wanted him to answer.

"What's a darkie like you doing in a Rebel uniform?"

After Bill explained whom he was and why he was a soldier, the man nodded and spit a mouthful of dark brown tobacco juice onto the rump of the closest mule. A disgusting dribble of the juice ran from the corner of his mouth and down into his beard, which he wiped with the back of his hand.

"Tobaccy juice keeps the horse flies from biting 'em on the arse," he said in order to justify spitting on the animal. "I've had many a rig git away from me when them danged flies decided to chomp down on the arse of a skittish horse or mule."

Following the advice of Captain Yopp, Bill did not tell the man about any of the people who had died in Virginia. He didn't want their families to learn the bad news from secondhand sources. When he finished telling the man everything he knew about the war in Virginia, the man told him all the news about the seaports being closed and the market dropping for cotton. He told Bill that one year ago he hauled four hundred pound bales of cotton to the train station in Dublin two or three times a day for six weeks during the harvest. Every wagonload would put a dollar in his pocket.

"Now that most of the menfolks are gone off to war and them Yankees are blockading the seaports and shipping lanes, there just ain't enough cotton being grown and shipped to give me but one load a day if I'm lucky. It's hurtin' my pocketbook something awful," the driver said. He spit again on the mule's rump.

The miles passed quickly. Before Bill knew it, the man had reined in the mules and was pointing down a long sandy road to a rambling farmhouse situated under a green dome of spreading oak trees. Bill knew the house because he had driven the Yopps' wagon to it several times to pick up Rafe for Thomas' hunting parties. Whitehall was less than five miles from here. Bill grimaced at the thought of what lay ahead of him before he could begin his final trek home.

After thanking the man for the ride, the young soldier jumped from the big wagon. He began walking down the mile–long narrow road. A mid afternoon breeze was swirling along the dusty ruts of the lane, making small whirlwinds that shook the broom straw grass and disappeared in the thick brambles. A crow cawed noisily to announce Bill's presence from his perch atop a skinny persimmon tree just off the road. Dead blackberry bushes and green honeysuckle vines covered both sides of the narrow road. Bill had removed his shoes. He enjoyed the feel of the soft Georgia dirt on his feet. It was obvious from the weeds on the road that few wagons had made their way to this house since Rafe had left for the war.

As he drew near the house he could barely make out the figure of Mrs. Pennington. She was in a long, gray, homespun dress, standing on the front porch, straining to see if the soldier walking down the road could be her husband. She shaded her eyes with her left hand and held her right hand up to her chest as if it would help to keep her heavy heart from racing so fast.

Several minutes passed before she saw that it was a black boy in a Confederate uniform. Then she recognized Bill and walked into the shady dirt yard to greet him. Several chickens squawked and scrambled out from underfoot as she walked toward him. An old yard dog barked and then went back to sleep. Dead sticks and limbs were haphazardly piled in the yard where the children had gathered what little firewood they could manage.

She had only covered ten or fifteen feet when a confusing thought crossed her mind. She realized Bill might be coming to bring bad news about Rafe. She stopped in her tracks and stood there, frozen and breathless, until he came within talking distance. He could sense her fright as he drew near her.

Alice Pennington was an attractive twenty–eight–year–old brunette with a tanned face and crystal blue eyes. Captain Yopp had always told Rafe that if he hadn't married her first she would have been a Yopp by now.

"Bill!" she called out with a weak smile and twisted brow. "What on earth are you doing out here? I thought you were in Virginy with the boys."

Bill waved a greeting and smiled as he removed his gray forage cap. He held it close to his chest.

"Afternoon, Mrs. Pennington," he said with a slight courteous bow. "I jes got home for a few days of furlough from the war, and Captain Yopp wanted me to come see you. Can we go up on your porch and get out of this sun?"

he nervously asked as he pointed toward the house. As he stood there, he could feel his heart beat in the sides of his neck and his chest tightening. So far, he was following Thomas' instructions to the letter.

As soon as Bill asked her to sit down, the tone of his voice and the jittery, nervous look in his eyes told that he was not bringing pleasant news. *Perhaps Rafe was wounded or was sick,* she thought.

Before they reached the porch, she turned to Bill and asked in a quivering voice, "Bill, is Rafe all right?"

Bill did not respond until she had seated herself in the old rocker. He stood near the porch railing with his hat in hand. He was shaking nervously and had trouble looking the beautiful young woman in the eyes.

"Miss Alice, Captain Yopp gave me a letter to give you, but since you can't read and I can't read yet, I took it to memory. Here is what the Captain wanted me to tell you."

Bill stared out across the weed–covered fields in front on the house, took a long deep breath, and began speaking in the monotone voice of a child reciting a poem from memory in front of his classmates.

Dear Alice,

It is with a heavy heart and sad bereavements that I must tell you that Rafe passed away on October 11 from the dysentery that has already killed seven other men of Company H. I was at Rafe's side constantly during his sickness, and he wanted me to tell you that he loved you and the children. He said he was sorry he wouldn't be coming home. He was a brave man and good friend, and I miss him every minute of every day. I have given Bill fifteen dollars to give you, which was all the money that Rafe had. We will send his belongings home on the next wagon that heads south. He was buried in Lynchburg with the other boys by a real preacher with a full religious ceremony. I expect their bodies will be sent home shortly after the war for proper burial. If you are in need of anything, please ask Bill to help you. We will send someone from Whitehall to see to you and the children. My heart breaks for you.

With much sadness I remain very sincerely,
Thomas Yopp, Captain CSA

Bill took a deep breath, reached into his pocket, and slowly removed the yellowing envelope. After looking at it, he held it out to the young woman. She was in complete shock and had not spoken a word. Her only sound had been an audible gasp of distress when Bill had recited the first sentence.

Her eyes were glassy and her hands trembled uncontrollably as she slowly reached out to take the letter from Bill. Then, without warning, she quickly drew her hand back before taking it as if Rafe's death would not be real if she never held the envelope. Finally, after several seconds of staring at the message of death, she reached forward again and took the letter. She brought it close to her heart and held it there. She closed her eyes and leaned her head back on the rocker. The largest tears Bill had ever seen erupted from the corners of her eyes.

"Miss Alice," Bill said in a soft voice, "I done stopped at your mama's house in Dublin this morning and told her the sad news. She and your paw are coming right behind me to be with you and help out with the chilluns. They said they had to gather up some things and pack the wagon. I ain't told Rafe's parents, though, but I'll be glad to do that if you wants me to."

Alice slowly turned her head and looked at Bill. She wiped her cheeks with her apron and tried to present herself as composed and strong. Despite that, Bill could tell that she was dying inside.

"Thank you, Bill. You have been most kind to come all this way to bring me this sad news about my dear Rafe. We will be able to take care of everything ourselves," she said. She stiffened her jaw and wiped her nose and eyes again. "I will never forget your kindness and hope that when this war is over you will come back and visit. Also, please send my regards to Captain Yopp. Tell him I will be forever grateful for his thoughtfulness."

Bill looked curiously around the yard and fields before asking his next question.

"Miss Alice, I ain't seen any of the boys around here that used to help out Masr Rafe. Should I go get them to come be with you?"

"They all left shortly after Rafe went off to war," she replied. "We couldn't afford to own any slaves, and I didn't have the money to pay those boys to work any longer."

"How you been managin' things around here with no help?" he asked with a puzzled and concerned look on his face.

"My parents have been helping us, and we just live day by day, Bill," she said. She wiped her eyes again with the back of her hand.

Bill reached into his haversack and removed a small cloth bag.

"Here is Masr Rafe's money," he said. He placed the small cloth bag in her cold quivering hand.

"I hates to leave you, Miss Alice, but I better be going so I can get home to Whitehall before dark." He paused. "You sure you'll be all right 'til your folks get here?"

"Yes, Bill," she said, the tears continuing to flow down her cheeks. "We'll be just fine."

Bill heard the sound of children running and laughing inside the house. It made his heart even heavier. They would have to hear the sad news, too.

He walked from the porch. He had only taken a few steps when Alice called out to him.

"Bill, Captain Yopp's letter said there was fifteen dollars in this sack, but it looks like a heap more than that. Where did this extra money come from?"

Bill slowly turned around and smiled.

"The cap'n must have counted Masr Rafe's money wrong, Miss Alice. I'm sure that was what happened. I better be leaving now. Long way to walk this evenin'."

He tipped his hat and turned down the long, dusty lane. Once his head was facing away from her, a big tear slipped down his dark cheek and left a visible track to the point where it dropped from his jaw onto his jacket. Even though he was crying, he had a smile on his lips because he knew how the extra ten dollars had gotten into that small sack for Miss Alice. It made him feel better. He only had to shine one hundred pairs of shoes to earn that money, and there would be plenty of dirty boots waiting on him when he returned to Virginia.

He thought that she needed it much more than he did, and he was right.

YOU DON'T EVEN THROW A PROPER SHADOW

mber sunset shadows were scattering their cool fingers across the darkening late afternoon sky when Bill made his final turn onto the oak–lined road that led to Whitehall Plantation. His breath shortened as he stopped to take in the splendor and comfort of the scene. He had dreamed of this almost every night for the last several months. Before him stood a half–mile long sandy lane that was shaded by over forty majestic oaks. Twenty on either side of the lane formed an inviting cool tunnel that led to the warmth of the big, white house of the Yopp family. Glowing brass lanterns had already been lit on either side of the front door. That job that had been his for the past twelve years, and he wondered to himself who had been promoted to fill his shoes.

To his right, Bill could see across a thirty–acre cotton field still speckled with white remnants like snowflakes. He saw the distant roofs of the slave houses and the wispy plumes of a dozen dinner fires snaking upwards into the sunset sky. The smoke settled in a thin layer on top of the fields and looked like friendly early morning fog that kept things still and quiet. In the distance, he could hear the happy sounds of children playing tag or hide–and–go–seek. The unmistakable howl of a familiar old coon dog named Jimbo pierced the solitude. Bill knew his howl by heart. He smiled from ear to ear when he recognized his old companion. They had been on many enjoyable hunts together in the nearby forests. Jimbo didn't bark like this unless he had seen something he didn't like. He was more than likely barking at the old gray cat that belonged to Janie Yopp. The cat loved to upset the dogs and then scamper up a tree.

Off to the left he saw the ageless magnolia tree, where every generation of Yopp children and their friends had spent countless hours climbing to the top and imagining they were on the watchtower of some frontier fort. He guessed they had shot at least a thousand wild Indians from this tree during his childhood. He chuckled to himself at the notion.

Bill detoured off the main road. He was drawn under the magnolia's low hanging limbs and entered the shadowy, serene, private world of his childhood memories. His mind wandered to happier days when children laughed and played here, when none knew or cared that their skin was white or black or different from the other. They were just friends.

He slowly walked around the massive base of the tree until he found the carved initials, T.Y and B.Y., that Thomas had scratched in the bark many years ago. He traced each letter with his forefinger as if he were re–writing them. He could perfectly remember the day when Thomas had cut them into the smooth gray bark. Darkness closed in rapidly under the spreading tree, so

Bill slipped out through an opening in the low limbs that touched the ground. He was soon back in the lane.

With no forethought, he broke into a run and quickly found himself leaping up the front steps of the huge home. He knew that none of the slaves were allowed to use the front door, but he felt that tonight was special. He took a deep breath and continued. He nervously removed his cap and beat the dust off his jacket and pants with it. Then he reached up to the large brass knocker and rapped three times. Having never used the front door knocker, he was shocked at its loudness. The knocks resonated through his body and sounded as thunderous as a ten–pound iron sledge hitting a hollow cypress tree. It seemed like several minutes had gone by before he heard the footsteps of someone coming to the front door. A distinguished black man in a dark butler's suit pulled the big door open and began to say something to the boy in the dirty gray uniform.

"Colored folks don't come to the front—" he said, stopping in mid sentence when he recognized the grinning boy.

"Daddy, it's me, Bill," he said with a beaming smile.

His father stood paralyzed for a few moments. Then he lunged forward and embraced the boy so tightly that it almost took away Bill's breath.

"You is home! Thank you, Lord; my boy is home," William said loudly as he hugged him tightly again. He stepped back to look him over and then embraced him once more.

"Boy, you is as scrawny as an old sick dog. Have you not been eatin' right?"

"I got real sick last month and lost some weight. I'm still pretty puny from it all, but I'm feeling better every day."

The thought suddenly crossed William's mind that perhaps there were others with Bill. He looked around to see where they were. When he didn't see anyone, he turned back to Bill with a worried look.

"Where's Masr Thomas?"

"Oh, he couldn't come home right yet. Things is startin' to heat up in Virginy, and the colonel said Cap'n Thomas would have to wait a spell before he could take some leave. He gave me a couple of weeks to come home to get my strength and to see everyone. I been missin' y'all a heap," he said as he looked down and shuffled his feet.

As Bill and his father stood talking and hugging in the doorway, several of the teenage Yopp children raced down the stairs into the grand foyer. They recognized Bill and ran up to him calling his name. The boys patted Bill on the back and shook his hand. The girls grinned and told Bill how great it was to see him. He had never felt so loved.

Before long the entire household was calling out that Bill was at the front door. One by one they raced to greet him in the foyer. Margaret and Jeremiah were the next to arrive, and after a warm and excited welcome, they immediately asked about Thomas.

"Masr Thomas is jes fine," Bill said. He gave a big smile

and bowed his head out of habit. "I been takin' really good care of him for you. I'll have to sit down with all of y'all and tell you about everything that's going on in Virginy. But before I do, I think I might just get weak–kneed if I don't get something decent to fill my empty belly and rest a spell."

"Bill!" His mother screamed as she raced through the drawing room wiping her hands on her apron. "The children said it was you, but I thought they was foolin' with me likes they always do. Praise the good Lawd you is home," she said, tears streaming down her cheeks.

Once again Bill was hugged to the point of suffocation, but he felt the same way and embraced her just as hard.

"Lawdy boy, you is so skinny you don't even throw a proper shadow," his mother exclaimed as she squeezed his arm and inspected his drawn face. "Did I hear you been sick?"

"Yes, ma'am," Bill replied. "I'm as weak as three day old lettuce. Caught the dysentery. Cap'n Yopp said we got it from drinking bad water. It's a mighty powerful sickness, and it jumped on about five hundred of our boys, killing some of them. I was jes lucky, I suppose. Masr Thomas took good care of me the whole time I was feelin' badly."

"Well," his mother said, putting her hands on her hips, "you sho 'nuff come to the right place to get some meat back on your skinny bones. But first I think you need to get a proper scrubbin' and put on some fresh clothes. You smell like an old pole cat, and we don't want you to be stinkin' up Miss Margaret's house."

"Let's don't kill the boy before he even gets settled in," William said as he pulled Bill away from his wife. "Let's get him fed first and then you can scrub off what little skin he has left on these bones. When he's through with all of that, if he's still alive, then he can tell us all about what's going on up nawth."

"How long you goin' to be home?" William asked the boy. He affectionately placed his big hand on his son's shoulder.

Bill turned his palms up and answered, "I don't rightly know, Daddy. Masr Thomas said I could jes stay home if I wanted to. I needs to do some powerful thinking about this once I get rested up and strong again."

"Well, you jes do what you gots to do, Bill," his father said, giving a smile.

Bill turned to the master and his wife.

"Miss Margaret and Masr Jeremiah," he said, opening his haversack, "I brung you a letter from Masr Thomas. He said for me to tell you that it was a long letter and that he felt badly he had not written more often, but that after you find out what all we have been doin', you'll understand. Also, I needs to tell you some mighty awful news," he said. He dropped his head and nervously twisted his hat in his hands.

"Rafe Pennington got really sick and just up and died several weeks ago. I stopped at his house on my way home and told Miss Alice. I gave her a special letter from Masr

Thomas. I told her that y'all would be checking on her to see if she needs anything. Her helpers done left her, and other than her old folks in town, she ain't got nobody to look after her out on that big, lonely farm."

As soon as Bill said the words "Rafe Pennington died," the atmosphere of joy and jubilation changed to one of stark sadness and shock. Most people at Whitehall had known Rafe Pennington since he was a little boy. He was the first casualty of the Civil War that they had all known. The war suddenly became very real, very dangerous, and very close to home. Rafe had grown up on a neighboring farm and had been a fixture at Whitehall with Thomas almost every day until he started school. Bill's mother had often referred to Rafe as "one of her chillun" because he was always sneaking into the kitchen for a cookie or a slice of pie. She had prided herself in popping Rafe and Thomas on their behinds with her butter paddle more than one time, but she had never hit them hard enough to hurt.

Standing in the quiet candle light of the foyer, the older women shook their heads. Tears cascaded down their cheeks as the magnitude of the loss hit them. The men and young boys dropped their heads and said words of grief to each other. Jeremiah called for everyone, black and white, to join hands in a circle. He said a short prayer asking God to welcome Rafe into heaven and to watch over his family. He also used the occasion to ask for continued blessings and to bring Thomas home safely.

Everyone said their sad amens and continued holding

hands for nearly a minute longer. It made them feel safe to be connected to the larger group.

Through her tears and sniffles, the mistress took control of the situation. She spewed out a plan of action, something that had always been one of her strong points.

"Bill, that was a mighty fine thing you did today. Our entire family will forever be indebted to you for speaking with Alice Pennington and helping her out like you did. I have always known you would grow up to be a fine young man with a heart of gold, and you have not let me down."

Bill's heart swelled with pride at hearing these words from Miss Margaret.

She turned to the group of servants who were standing together as a family.

"Lia, first thing in the morning I'd like for you to put together a big basket of whatever food we can spare. Be sure to get one of those big hams from the smokehouse. Constance, we should take some of the children's old clothes down there," she said to Bill's fourteen–year–old sister. "Figure out what sizes they will need and show them to me before you pack them up."

She then turned to Bill's father.

"William, we'll need for you to drive us over there around nine in the morning. Also, William, why don't you go get one of the strong boys to go with us? He can cut some firewood for Alice and her children while we are there visiting. We're probably going to have some cool weather in the next week or so, and we don't want that poor girl to catch her death of cold."

Just like that, Miss Margaret had the whole situation under control.

—

The remainder of the evening was a whirlwind of eating, bathing, and talking. By the time Bill had finished "the best food he had eaten in months," word had spread throughout the slave quarters that he was home. Everyone had come up to the front of the big house to welcome him back. Jeremiah had suggested that Bill go out on the front porch and tell everyone all the news at one time. The attention gave Bill a feeling of pride and personal accomplishment. Over twenty slaves and their children sat down in the yard under the sprawling oaks and were completely silent when Bill began talking. The radiance of the lanterns reflected off their shiny dark faces. It filled him with joy to see all of his lifelong friends. He stood on the top step, while the Yopp family sat in the rocking chairs behind him and on either side of the wide porch. The evening was a little cool, so most women wore their shawls. The men had on their jackets and hats.

Jeremiah stood up first. He welcomed everyone and explained what a joyous occasion it was to have Bill back from the war. He turned to Bill and asked him to share the news about the adventures he and Thomas had experienced since their departure over three months earlier. Bill took a step forward and nodded his appreciation to

Jeremiah before he began talking. He had on fresh clean clothes, but he still held on to his gray forage cap.

"Before I get into what all we have been doing in the war, I wanted all of you to know I ain't never missed nothing in my life like I missed you, my friends and family." Bill paused. He almost got choked up with emotion as he looked down at the soft cap and twisted it nervously in his hands.

"This is home, and it means something very special to me. If any of you folks thinks that life is better in other places, let me tell you right now that I ain't seen it yet, and I've seen lots of this country in the last few months. Cap'n Yopp sends his regards to all of you. He is doing fine and ain't been sick nearly a day since we left. He said he hopes to be comin' home around Christmas for a few days if the fightin' ain't too bad."

Bill paused and took a deep breath as he prepared to tell more news.

"I brung some bad news home with me that all of you needs to know about. A whole bunch of our boys died a couple of weeks ago from the dysentery sickness, and a bunch of them is still staring death in the face. Cap'n Yopp said eight had died, and he supposed another five or six might go soon. We ain't lost but a few men in any fights yet, but this sickness was something terrible. I heard the doctor say that over five hundred men from our regiment was laid up with it."

A groan of sadness swept through the group of slaves. Bill heard prayers being said by many of them.

Bill continued talking for nearly an hour. He told the group almost everything that Company H had experienced and where they had been. Several times, Jeremiah had to remind him to get back on track when he started giving vivid descriptions of the countryside, the mountains, and the foliage in West Virginia and Virginia.

"I don't think tonight is the best time for geography lessons, Bill. Just tell us the news from the war," Jeremiah said. He gave Bill a cordial smile. "Anyone who wants to hear about the trees and mountains can ask you about that later." Bill's mother chuckled. She knew that once Bill started talking he was likely to talk 'til the cows come home if somebody didn't rein him in.

Bill nodded his nervous agreement and continued with the news for a while longer. Jeremiah and his wife interrupted him several times. They were asking specific questions, which he gladly answered. Shortly after that, the slaves began posing their questions to him about life in the army. They wanted to know what it was like marching into battle. They were all silent and spellbound by his firsthand accounts.

Toward the end of Bill's explanation, one of the middle–aged black men stood up and asked Bill a question.

"Bill, tell us what you is hearin' about the slaves being freed and what they is doin' once they get their papers."

Jeremiah and his wife cut their eyes toward each other with an anxious glance. They were curious, too, but were hopeful this would not lead to problems with the slaves.

Without any hesitation, Bill began his answer.

"One thing that truly surprised me was how many colored folks there are in the army. As you probably know, coloreds can't be fighters. They can be jes about anything else in the army, and there are lots of jobs. It's hard work, but it ain't no harder than what you been doin' on the farm. And the best part is that they pays you to work."

The older man looked at Bill with a puzzled face. Just about everyone on the lawn began whispering about what he had just said.

"You mean they pays you to be in the army? Even the coloreds?"

"Yes, suh," Bill replied. "I been makin' about ten dollars a month, and some of the boys who is higher than a private get more than that." He paused.

"Now as far as what's happening to the freed slaves, I can't rightly tell you much. I heard some of the officers saying that some slaves have run off and tried to join the Yankee Army, but they jes sends them home when they find out they is runaways. I don't understand that since the Yankees say they is fightin' to give us freedom. Why would they send these colored boys back home to a place they didn't want to be? I met some folks in Atlanta who had left their farms and were trying to scratch out a living in the city, but they was having a hard time. Lots of them jes come on back home after a while because they know they can get a hot meal and a roof over their heads when they are home."

Finally the late night yawns turned into restlessness. Many of the people began to excuse themselves so that they could pick this up another day. Others were getting too cold to sit outside any longer, so they just bundled up and drifted off into the darkness.

"It's been a day to remember," Jeremiah said to Bill as he stood up. He put his hand forward to shake Bill's. Jeremiah was very appreciative that Bill had shared the details of his adventures with everyone.

"I know you must be dog tired after your journey. You get a good night's sleep, and we'll see you tomorrow and talk about any news that you forgot to mention tonight."

—

Bill had been home less than a week when the first faint twinge of guilt began streaking through his mind and gnawing at his gut. By the end of his second week, these feelings had intensified to a constant concern. For some reason, he could not get his mind off Thomas, the men from Laurens County, or the excitement and adventure he had experienced with them. Each night as he lay in bed and each morning when he awoke, he would imagine what his friends were doing. Were they fighting or marching? Were they sitting around the fire singing his favorite songs? Had anyone else gotten sick, and did they need his help? Who was cooking for Thomas?

Bill thrived on hard work and staying productive, but everyone at Whitehall was being overly protective and sensitive to him. Once again his days at home had become routine and monotonous. He was told to sleep as late as he would like and eat plenty of food to regain his strength. Whenever he was up at dawn to help with the chores, he was scolded for not taking care of himself.

It was a chilly starlit night, and Bill was enjoying sitting alone on his favorite stool beside the crumbling orange coals of the campfire. All the children were asleep, and the older folks were doing their final chores of the day. As he leaned back and gazed up at the stars, his father walked out and sat down beside him.

"Son, you ain't quite been yourself the last few days. Are you feelin' okay?" William asked in a very concerned and sincere tone. He took a seat on a nearby bench. He pulled out a corncob pipe and lit it with a flaming twig from the fire pit.

"I feel jes fine, Daddy," Bill said. He smiled. "I jes got lots on my mind," he continued in a somber tone as he looked down at the coals and poked them with a long stick. When he did, sparkling embers that reminded Bill of fireflies fluttered quickly into the ink colored sky until they flickered out and disappeared.

Bill's eyes reflected the glow of the fire as his father looked at him.

"Well, I think that maybe we needs to be talkin' about what's on your mind. Maybe my older head can share some wisdom with you, if I still got any left."

Bill turned and smiled respectfully at his father. Then, as he looked back at the coals, his brow wrinkled into a serious gaze. His eyes were fixated on the flames in such a frozen stare that William became even more concerned.

There was a long pause of silence with the only sounds

being the crackle of the fire and the haunting calls of two distant hoot owls talking to each other.

Bill suddenly took in a deep breath and turned to face his father's searching eyes.

"Daddy, I been feelin' like I needs to get back up to Virginy with Thomas and the other boys. I'm feelin' fine now. My strength is back, and I know they needs me."

William did not reply immediately but simply nodded his head in agreement. He had already speculated that this was what was on Bill's mind. His son had experienced a taste of the boundless and exciting world outside of Whitehall, and he wanted more. He longed for the adventure, the freedom, and the education that the army offered. He wanted to taste them again. He had seen the leaves change to crimson and gold in the Virginia mountains and watched the fog as it slithered through creek bottoms in late afternoon pastures. He longed to see it all again. Most importantly, he had experienced the feeling of self–importance and self–worth, something that no slave he had ever known had been allowed to experience, and he had to have more.

—

As the noisy locomotive pulled slowly from the Dublin station four days later, Bill stood on the rear of the passenger car and waved goodbye to his teary–eyed parents.

His life was about to change from peace and tranquility to war and death.

DYING BECAME A PART OF LIVING

The first winter of the war for Bill's company consisted of long weary marches, endless days in drafty boxcars, miserable living in freezing muddy valleys, constant stomach and intestinal problems, and waking up each day with nothing more to look forward to than more of the same. The poor weather also brought with it an increasing number of illnesses such as pneumonia, whooping cough, tuberculosis, measles, chicken pox, and dysentery that killed the boys off more quickly than any battle. Because most of these boys had grown up in the relative isolation of a distant farm, most had never encountered these diseases and had no immunities to them.

Almost daily the sound of Taps being bugled for some departed soul could be heard somewhere in the huge encampment. As the months marched by, the soldiers became more hardened to the trumpet sounds that signaled the passing of another comrade. Few paid it any attention by the summer of 1862. Dying had become a part of living for each of them. These boys had no idea that by the end of the war, two out of every three soldiers who died would succumb to the ravages of disease rather than battle wounds. To die in a coughing, feverish fit in a cold and lonely tent was hardly a fitting end for these valiant patriots.

The regiment gradually moved from western Virginia to join forces with the massive Army of Northern Virginia in Fredericksburg, the strategic city that lay halfway between Richmond and Washington, D.C. After only a short time there, the regiment was dispatched to Yorktown, as the Confederate forces continued to build their strength for a push into Washington and the other states of the Union. Bill and Thomas frequently talked late into the night about the ominous signs that the truly big battles were soon to begin. There was little talk of this among the men, but everyone knew that their days of waiting and preparation for battle would end soon.

By the end of May 1862, the Union Army of the Potomac, roughly one hundred thousand men, had pushed southward to within twelve miles of Richmond. It was a grand plan that Abe Lincoln hoped would bring a quick end to the foolish rebellion. A deadly cat–and–mouse game between the Union and Confederate armies ensued until the morning of May 31, when over eighty four thousand men rammed into each other at a bloody railroad junction called Fair Oaks Station, Virginia.

It was a cool, clear morning when the Richmond defense forces turned the tables on the Union troops and launched a hellish offense at Fair Oaks. Thus, the battle of what would later be called "Seven Pines" began. It would be one of the bloodiest of the war for both armies. Before it ended twenty–four hours later, over 13,700 men would become casualties. Nearly six hundred men per hour were cut down in the fierce battle.

Bill's company moved into a holding position on a hill just north of Fair Oaks. For the first time since the war began, Bill could see the endless blue ranks of Yankees as they massed on the distant tree lines. In the past, they had strained their eyes to see Union cavalrymen race behind a hill, or they would catch a glimpse of a hit–and–run band of Yankee foot soldiers off across some green field. They had also witnessed long columns of Yankee prisoners being herded south to a notorious prison called Andersonville in the western part of Georgia. Occasionally Bill's company had even been involved in minor skirmishes, but today would christen all of these men in the grisly blood bath of a major battle.

"I ain't never seen so many Yankees in one place in my life," Bill said in a fearful tone to Captain Yopp. They were standing on a rocky outcropping surveying the situation in the valley below.

"I'm guessing that when the order comes, we'll be marching down this hill and will hit those boys head on," Thomas said in a solemn tone.

The tense hours crawled by endlessly until finally a fast galloping courier from battalion headquarters raced up and issued orders to the company commanders. All up and down the line, officers could be heard calling out battle orders to their men. Within minutes, the bugles were sounding. Bill began beating his attack march as loudly as he had ever heard it played. Over the 'Prepare for Battle' roll of the drums and the piercing calls of the bugles, Bill could hear a crescendo of sound building around him. It spread like a wave through the woods and sounded like a thousand wagon drivers prodding their beasts to move out with their heavy loads. The sound was the infamous Rebel Yell that brought fear into the hearts of all enemies who heard it and instilled courage and pride into the men who voiced it.

Bill looked down the long gray line and then back at Thomas, who had raised his sword toward the enemy and began calling out loudly, "For your homes and your sweethearts. Forward for Georgia!"

Bill and dozens of drummers with other companies struck up the long rolling battle rhythm and began leading the troops slowly down the hill. The line of Confederate soldiers stretched as far as he could see. He hurried to keep up with Thomas, who was on horseback. Every time Bill looked up at Thomas, he was busy motioning orders to the various squads and platoons of the company.

Soon the booming noise of Confederate cannon fire was heard in their rear as the steel balls streaked overhead and threw up huge clouds of black dirt, white smoke, and certain death in the midst of the Union soldiers. Bill was amazed that he could occasionally actually see the big cannon balls flying over his head. He followed their flight and watched as they created death among the blue suited soldiers.

As the command to open fire began rippling along the lines, Bill saw Thomas turn and look straight at him with a deadly serious stare on his face. Immediately he motioned with his sword to Bill to move to the rear of the advancing ranks.

"Cap'n," Bill called out above the firing and yelling, "my place is up here with you, leadin' these boys to gets them Yankees. I don't belong in the rear."

For the first time in Bill's life, Thomas reeled his horse around and lost his temper with him.

"Bill, that is a direct order," Thomas called out loudly in a harsh voice. "Remove yourself to the rear of the advancing line and continue your drumming. Do you understand me?"

Without saying another word, Bill remorsefully turned around and made his way through the onslaught of soldiers who were running, firing, and dying. He understood that Thomas was sending him to the rear for his protection, but he felt his place was in the front with the captain. By now, the noise was so deafening that at times Bill could not even hear his own drum beats.

Bill came up over a small ridge, and suddenly he could see the entire battlefield of gray and blue waves of men racing toward each other. Puffs of smoke hung like low clouds over the valley. Squads and companies of soldiers on both sides were stopping and shooting in unison. It sounded as if someone had set off a thousand strings of firecrackers on the Fourth of July. The flame and smoke from their muskets was blinding.

Then it happened.

While standing on the ridge, he searched frantically

for Thomas but could not see him anywhere. Suddenly he saw a riderless horse, Thomas' stallion, racing off to the right flank. Bill knew immediately that Thomas had either fallen from his stallion or had been shot from the saddle. With not so much as an afterthought, Bill dropped his drum and sticks and raced back through the advancing line to search for his master. The bloody field was quickly becoming littered with gray suited bodies and screaming men as he trotted a zigzag course toward the valley. He looked to his right and saw Bill Johnson from his company. He raced to him, asking if he had seen the captain.

"He went down over yonder," Johnson answered loudly while nodding his head to the right. Both of his hands were busily working to reload his rifle as he forcefully shoved his ramrod down the barrel. Bullets zipped and zinged all around Bill. One even brushed his jacket sleeve and left a small groove of torn threads.

His eyes searched frantically in the direction Johnson had pointed, and he quickly saw a crumpled body in a gray officer's uniform sprawled on the littered field. It was Thomas. He wasn't moving. A spreading circle of blood saturated his uniform jacket on the upper part of his chest.

"Cap'n! Cap'n!" Bill screamed as he knelt beside Thomas and lifted his head up from the ground. "You can't die on me!" the boy yelled as he shook Thomas' motionless body. A cannon shell exploded nearby and blew up a wave of dirt and rocks in all directions. The concussion threw Bill ten feet away from Thomas. Bill did not know how long he had been unconscious, but when his head cleared, he checked his body and was grateful that he had not been severely wounded. Blood from several cuts on his forehead streamed into his eyes. Through smoke and fire, he slowly crawled back to where Thomas lay.

As Bill sat holding his master's head in his lap, the young captain's eyes fluttered. He slowly began moaning in pain. Thomas moved his right hand over to touch the wet patch of blood on his jacket.

With dirt and blood caked on his face and tears streaming down his cheeks, Bill smiled one of the widest grins of his life.

"You going to be just fine, Cap'n. Bill is here to look after you. I ain't lettin' no Yankee get his hands on you." He peered through the white smoke of battle. The smell of burning gunpowder infiltrated every thread in every piece of cloth on the field. Suddenly Bill felt a wave of nausea float through his body. He took a deep breath, drawing in his courage and determination, and soon felt better.

Bill opened Thomas' jacket and could see the small crimson hole where the lead ball had neatly punched through his body just below his shoulder. It appeared that it had missed the bones and had come cleanly out the back. He ripped his own shirt off and began packing it up against the wounds to stop the bleeding.

"We got to get out of here, Cap'n," Bill screamed loudly in Thomas' ear as he looked at the raging battle that was only one hundred yards down the valley from them. Dirt, grass, and flesh were being thrown high into the air from the cannon shell explosions. Soon Bill and Thomas were covered with the sickening waste of battle.

Thomas drunkenly struggled to his feet while holding onto Bill's shoulder. They began slowly climbing the hill to safety. They had walked no more than fifty yards when Bill looked back over his shoulder and saw a cannon shell explode in the exact spot where the captain had fallen. Thomas saw it as well and gave Bill a weak smile as he labored to keep moving up the ridge. He was amazed at the powerful arms and shoulders that Bill used to support him. He had never realized Bill was this strong.

"Help us! Over here!" Bill screamed to the litter bearers who were beginning to filter down the hill to pick up any wounded soldiers they could find without risking their own lives. Bullets were still zipping through the air and thumping into the ground and nearby trees, so Bill tried to stay low while moving forward with Thomas. Two litter bearers saw the struggling men and raced down the ridge. They quickly placed Thomas on the stretcher. Within minutes they had taken him up to the ridge road where the ambulance wagons were waiting to take the wounded to the field hospital.

Bill helped the driver haul Thomas into the rear of the wagon that was already crowded with dead and dying soldiers. He gingerly placed Thomas' head in his lap and held a bloody rag over the wound in an effort to stop the bleeding. Thomas drifted in and out of consciousness. He had a gray look of death on his bloody face that frightened Bill beyond anything he had ever experienced.

Bill never quit mumbling, "you goin' to be all right, Masr. You goin' to be all right."

Bill had been so engrossed in Thomas' welfare that he had paid little attention to the gruesome spectacle around him inside the wagon. Six gravely injured men were lying in the wagon. Each of them was covered in blood. Swarms of big green flies hovered over each person, and Bill tried to shoo them away by waving his arms. Thomas groaned in semi-conscious pain each time Bill moved, so he just left the flies to their feast.

One man's arm was missing just above his right elbow and blood spurted from the ragged stump as he screamed in agony. The panic-stricken young ambulance driver called to a shell-shocked soldier walking down the road to help the wounded man, but the zombie-like soldier just turned and wandered into the woods, dragging his rifle butt on the ground. Seconds later the spurting blood ceased. Bill saw the man take his final breath. Another man was moaning loudly from a wound in his belly. Bill knew from camp talk that this man would surely die. The floor of the wagon soon became a sticky pool of blood, but Bill hardly noticed because he was so focused on Thomas.

—

The first week of June 1862 at Howard's Grove Hospital in Richmond was a nightmare of pain, screaming, and nausea for Thomas. He had lost a considerable amount of blood, and his wound had the early signs of infection, which generally spelled death. The doctors and nurses treated his wound with iodine and carbolic acid in an attempt to stem the infection.

When Thomas was first carried into the field surgeon's tent, Bill saw waist high tables covered with bleeding and screaming men. Surgeons were sawing off arms and legs with frightful frequency, throwing the mangled body parts on a pile nearby. Bill was so covered in blood from his wagon ride that the hospital staff was certain he was mortally wounded and tried unsuccessfully to pull him onto a surgical table. As he waited on the surgeons to finish with Thomas, he was forced to run outside on more than one occasion to vomit what little food or moisture was left in his stomach. He had never seen so much blood or death in one place.

—

Bill had not slept in days. He sat groggily beside Thomas' bed and tried to take care of his every need. He wiped Thomas' sweaty brow with cool wet towels, spoke words of encouragement even though he was sure Thomas was not completely conscious, and fed him what little food he could take. A nurse had shown Bill how to care for the wound and keep the bandages changed because the hospital staff was so overwhelmed by the incoming war casualties. Gradually the combination of youth, cleanliness, and the caring touch of Bill and the hospital staff allowed Thomas to begin his recovery.

During the long days when Thomas drifted in and

out of consciousness, Bill began running errands for the nurses and helping the injured soldiers. Bill learned first aid quickly, and it soon became evident to the medical staff that the young black man had a special touch when caring for the patients. Bill could be found wandering the hospital long after Thomas had gone to sleep at night. He stopped to cheer up wounded soldiers, get them some water, or change their dressings. One of the doctors even tried to convince Bill to transfer from his company to the hospital staff, but Bill graciously rejected the offer.

Bill had witnessed so many horrible sights since the day Thomas had been wounded that each time he closed his eyes he saw the same gruesome nightmares of death. He felt certain he would never be able to sleep soundly again. He had seen firsthand the ravages caused by the dreadful heavy lead bullets shot from the Yankee muskets. These bullets tore enormous wounds on impact. It was such a heavy projectile that an abdominal or head wound was usually fatal, and a hit to an extremity usually shattered any bone encountered.

—

By late June, Thomas was on the mend. The doctors were telling him that he needed to be removed from the hospital to make room for more serious cases. He had written his first letter home since the battle and hoped his family knew that he was in good hands with Bill. The doctors approved for Thomas to ride in a wagon, so Bill demanded that he take him back home to Dublin for his recuperation. The doctor had estimated that with good care, good food, and plenty of rest, he should be able to return to active duty within ninety days.

Thus the long hot trip back to Laurens County, Georgia, began with Bill driving an emaciated old mule on a dilapidated wagon. They traveled several hundred miles down into North Carolina until they could find a southbound train heading to Atlanta. Thomas had very little strength and was forced to try to sleep in the back of the bouncing wagon whenever possible. When it rained, Bill would park under a tree and gingerly move Thomas underneath the wagon to wait out the storm. Bill would hold his jacket over his master the whole time in an effort to keep him as dry as possible.

Most afternoons Bill would stop at homes along the roads and ask for food and water for his wounded master. In spite of the poverty that was sweeping the south, most people were anxious to help injured soldiers any way they could. On many nights, the good Samaritans would welcome Thomas into their homes and let him sleep in their beds while they slept on the floor. It was one small patriotic thing they could do to support the war effort and the boys fighting. Bill was thrilled because he was offered fresh piles of hay to sleep upon in the barns. After sleeping outdoors for so many months, he preferred the barns to many of the stuffy houses.

After thirteen days of hard traveling, Bill and Thomas arrived at Whitehall in a wagon they had rented in Dublin. There were great celebrations on the farm for several days after their two sons had come home. Bill was especially proud that he had finished reading his first book that week. He sat down to show his parents his new skill. Tears rolled down Lia and William's cheeks as they sat beside him and heard him proudly read wonderful stories from a tattered book. Bill had found the book on the battlefield, dropped by a Union soldier.

The doting women of Whitehall pampered Thomas to the point of irritation. Once again Bill became bored with that lifestyle and was anxious to get back to Virginia. It was not until September of 1862 that Captain Yopp felt strong enough to return to battle. Then he and Bill said their sad goodbyes, and the two friends, master and slave, made the long trek to Virginia.

THE DARK ANGEL . . .

Sometime during the second week in October, Captain Yopp and Bill caught up with their regiment in northern Virginia. It was a joyous reunion with hours of backslapping and storytelling about the trials and tribulations of their companions since Bill and Thomas had left. While they were in Georgia, the regiment had been involved in several hellish battles at Malvern Hill, Cedar Run, Manassas, and Harper's Ferry. There were missing friends and new faces in the company. It took a few days for Bill and Thomas to get over the shock of finding that several close friends had been killed.

Bill was saddened to tears when he learned that his friend and teacher, Josiah Bellflower, had taken a rifle shot between the eyes in a recent skirmish. Josiah had spent countless hours in the trenches with Bill, helping him to hone his reading and writing skills. Through it all they had become close friends. That night Bill sat down and wrote a long letter to Josiah's widow explaining what a wonderful friend he had been and that each word in his letter had a part of Josiah in it.

For the remainder of Bill's life, on the anniversary of Josiah's death, he wrote a letter to Josiah's wife and children. Each letter was written to remind the children, and later his grandchildren, what a wonderful man Josiah had been. He had given Bill the priceless gift of reading and writing, for which Bill was eternally grateful.

—

Embarrassed by the Northern Army's repeated failures and apparent lack of commitment in prosecuting the war, President Lincoln replaced his commanding general on November 7. This new regime, under General Ambrose Burnside, immediately launched a winter campaign against the Confederate capital of Richmond. He elected to get there by way of Fredericksburg, a strategically important town on the Rappahannock River.

The Union Army of the Potomac, now numbering over one hundred and ten thousand fighters, raced to Fredericksburg, arriving on November 17. There were only a few thousand Confederates on hand to challenge them, yet the Northern army advance came to a grinding halt on the eastern bank of the Rappahannock, opposite Fredericksburg. Upon their arrival, bitterly cold weather blew in, and heavy fog eerily shrouded the entire city and river bottom for days on end. The Union campaign was delayed for over a week when material the general had ordered for pontoon bridges failed to arrive. Disappointed by the delay, Burnside marked time for another two weeks. Meanwhile, General Lee took advantage of the stalled push to concentrate and entrench the Army of Northern Virginia, some seventy eight thousand strong, on the high ground behind Fredericksburg.

Some soldiers swore that these three weeks were the most miserable of their lives. They worked all day in the snow and bitter wind as they dug trenches, stacked heavy rocks, cut logs, and built gun emplacements. At night when the temperatures dipped below freezing and the snow softly pelted the ground, they slept huddled around fires or shivered inside small, drafty tents. Many men had no more than a single blanket to wrap themselves in. A low layer of smoke from the thousands of campfires in the valley hung like a veil of darkness over the troops. The smoke, combined with the constant heavy fog, created an end–of–the–world landscape that transformed the entire valley into a surreal and gloomy portrait of doom.

With the arrival of the pontoons, the Federals traversed the river on December 11 under the cover of dense fog, in spite of fierce fire from Confederate snipers concealed in buildings along the city's riverfront. When the Confederates finally withdrew from the wreckage of Fredericksburg, the Federal soldiers looted the town. By December 13, the Federals were prepared to launch a two–pronged attack to drive Lee's forces from a commanding set of hills just outside the city. That's where Bill and his company were deeply entrenched, along with almost eighty thousand other Confederate soldiers.

The main Union assault struck south of the city. Misunderstandings and slipshod leadership on the part of the commander of the Federals limited the attacking force to two small divisions: Major General George G. Meade to lead, and Major General John Gibbon in support. Meade's troops broke through an unguarded gap in the Confederate lines near the men of Bill's location, but fierce fighting expelled the unsupported Federals, inflicting heavy losses. The battle was ferocious with hand–to–hand fighting and rivers of blood.

The Union army launched its second attack from Fredericksburg against the Confederates left on Marye's Heights. Wave after wave of Federal attackers were cut down by Confederate troops firing from an unassailable position in a sunken road protected by a stone wall. Over the course of the afternoon of December 13, no fewer than fourteen successive Federal brigades of one thousand men each charged the hot, bloody wall of Confederate fire. Not a single Federal soldier reached the stone wall.

Bill's company found itself dug in within a dense forest area on the right flank of the Confederate forces as thousands upon thousands of Union soldiers raced from the valley plains up into the forests in an effort to flank the Confederate lines. Captain Yopp, Bill, and the other soldiers of the unit stayed hunkered down behind the log and dirt embankments they had built over the last three weeks. They fired their muskets at will as the unending procession of Yankee soldiers marched to their deaths.

Hearing a soldier laugh aloud and brag that "this was like shooting fish in a barrel," Captain Yopp raced into the pit, pulled the soldier up by his collar, and screamed. "Those are the bravest men in this battle, young man. Don't get too cocky because tomorrow it could be us on the other side of that wall. Just do your job and keep your mouth shut." The men knew Thomas was right and respected him for keeping them focused on the job at hand.

With his naked eye, Thomas could clearly see the next brigade of Union soldiers that was massing a half–mile down the hill. Thousands of dead and dying soldiers lay scattered on the sloping battlefield, yet new troops continued forming in groups on the plain below, preparing for the next attack. The men shook their heads in disbelief that the Union commanders could so foolishly continue to send their troops into the deathly fire that their regiment was unleashing. They tried to imagine the horror and hopelessness that the newest wave of Union soldiers must be feeling as they prepared to march to certain death.

During the pauses between firing, the boys behind the walls would drink water, eat what little food they could find, replenish their ammunition, and pray. During one of these afternoon lulls, Bill and the other soldiers could plainly hear the wounded Union soldiers moaning in anguished cries for help or a drink of water. Their calls for help were very unsettling to all of the men who could only imagine the horror that these fallen men must be experiencing.

One of the young Yankee soldiers lay dying from a stomach wound less than seventy–five yards down the hill from where Bill sat. He had listened to his suffering cries and seen the teenager's bloody face for the past thirty minutes. Finally, without saying anything to his comrades, Bill grabbed a full canteen, leaped over the log wall, and

raced down the hill to the soldier. Union soldiers down
the hill saw their chance for an easy kill, and dozens of
rifles fired in the direction of the drummer boy. Several of
Bill's friends screamed at him to come back, but he didn't
respond. The bullets zipped around him, kicking dirt into
his face, as he raced down the battle–scarred hill toward
the suffering soldier. Bill's Confederate comrades held
their breath, and the Union soldiers down the hill slowly
stopped firing when they realized what was happening.

Bill sat on the ground, raised the young Yankee soldier's blood–spattered head into his lap, and poured the
cool water between his parched lips. He then wet down
a rag and wiped the blood from the boy's tear–streaked
face as he told him that everything would be all right.
Up and down the blue and gray lines, more and more
men became aware of what Bill was doing. Gradually the
entire front stopped firing as they waited for him to complete his noble task. The battlefield grew eerily quiet as no
one spoke a word. Ten Cent Bill had done what most of
them wished they had the courage to do; he had shown
some compassion for these fallen heroes. The young boy
died in Bill's arms, but not before he looked into Bill's
eyes and thanked him.

When Bill climbed slowly back over the wall, he sat
down on a barrel and cried. Up and down the lines, a
roaring cheer came up like a howling wind as the men on
both sides showed their respect for Bill's act of kindness.
One by one a steady stream of his friends and admirers
walked up to him and shook his hand, telling him what

a good thing he had done. Thomas was the last to come. He patted Bill affectionately on the back and told him that God would always remember what he had done for that boy.

Bill's response was simple and sincere.

"I would've done it fer any of you, and you would've done it fer me."

They all knew he meant what he said.

That experience and his earlier days in the camp hospital with Thomas had changed Bill. He had discovered something extremely gratifying deep inside himself that he only felt when he helped wounded or dying men. On at least a dozen other occasions before the war's end, Bill was seen crawling across raging battlefields to bring comfort to the dying men who were making the ultimate sacrifice. For years after the conclusion of the war, men who had witnessed Bill's heroic Samaritan actions kindly referred to him as "The Dark Angel of Company H." Some of the soldiers felt that Bill was "blessed" because he had never been shot during his mercy missions. Soldiers would often come by and shake Bill's hand before a battle hoping some of his good luck would rub off on them.

—

Before each charge, the Federal artillery would fire dozens of shells up the ridge in hopes of weakening the Confederate defenses. Cannon shells were blasting treetops, and within two hours the forest looked as if a massive fire had removed everything that was green. The stench of gunpowder and burning underbrush penetrated every inch of the soldiers' bodies. Bill saw several men die when falling trees dropped directly on their entrenchment.

During this final artillery barrage, a cannon shell exploded in mid air just above the position where Thomas was standing. It peppered his body with hot shrapnel. He was blasted to the ground by the concussion and knocked unconscious. Once again Bill rushed to his rescue. With the help of several other boys, Thomas' motionless, bloody body was quickly rushed to the field hospital, with Bill hovering over him like a mother hen.

Captain Yopp had experienced a severe concussion from the blast and remained in a coma for over a week. The doctors assured Bill that Thomas' pulse was strong and his color was improving, but he still had not come out of the dream state. Bill began having serious concerns that Thomas might not survive, or if he did, he would be forced out of the service. If either of these situations happened, he was unsure and confused about what course of action he would take.

On December 15, the beaten Union army retreated across the Rappahannock. The Union had lost thirteen thousand soldiers in that harvest of death. The dreadful carnage was matched only by its futility. Federal morale plummeted, and once again, an angry President Lincoln swiftly relieved the commanding general. By contrast, the morale of the Confederacy reached a peak. Their casualties had been considerably lighter than the Union's, totaling only five thousand. Lee's substantial victory at

Fredericksburg, won with relative ease, increased the already buoyant confidence of the Army of Northern Virginia, which subsequently led to the invasion of the North the following summer.

—

As Thomas lay in the hospital, Bill approached the colonel who was in charge of the large medical camp.

"Colonel Roberts, suh," Bill said, standing at attention, "my name is Bill Yopp. I am here with Captain Thomas Yopp who was wounded several days back. I want to know what I can do to help out around here while I wait on the captain to get over his injuries."

The haggard colonel was surprised to see a volunteer since they usually had to draft men out of line companies to assist at the hospital.

"That is mighty nice of you to offer to help Private Yopp," the white haired colonel said. "Why don't you work with the nurses and help take care of the needs of the wounded men? They can use all the help you can give them."

"Yes, suh," Bill replied, nodding his head. "I will do jes that. I have had some experience over in Richmond in the hospital and enjoy helping out our boys."

Bill paused and smiled. "And suh, I'm a pretty fair cook. If you want a good meal one night, you jes come see me. I'll make you a dinner like your mama used to cook."

The colonel took an immediate liking to Bill and thought of his tempting offer all day. That night he surprised Bill by taking him up on his proposition. In spite of the short notice, Bill managed to come up with corn bread, bacon, beans with onions, and some of his good coffee. Because of this new friendship, Bill had ensured that Thomas would receive extra attention while in the hospital, which had been his motivation all along.

Thomas slipped in and out of his fog–like coma for twelve days. He was on the verge of death from dehydration when he finally awoke on the thirteenth day. It took almost three weeks of intensive care by Bill and the staff before Thomas became his old self again. Shortly thereafter, he was shipped to a more permanent hospital far behind the lines for his final stage of recuperation. Because Thomas was assured of an easy recovery, Bill was ordered by the replacement company commander to return to the unit. While this did not please him, he understood his place and knew that Thomas would be in good hands. During the remainder of Thomas' stay in the hospital, Bill wrote letters to him two or three times a week and kept him updated on everything the company was doing.

This was only the second time in Bill's life that he had been separated from his friend.

THE DEEPENING TWILIGHT
OF THE CONFEDERACY

Bill's regiment settled in for the long, northern Virginia winter of 1862–1863 and saw no major action for the next four months. Captain Yopp recuperated from his wounds and returned to the unit before March. The weary soldiers worked to survive each day. By the spring of 1863, the original 14ᵗʰ Regiment had been reduced to less than four hundred men, down from over one thousand men when they left Laurens County in July of 1861. As the winter turned to spring and the spring into summer, the men became invigorated. They were anxious for a fight. Most of all, they wanted to get this ugly and gruesome war over with so they could go home.

In June, Robert E. Lee decided it was time to bring the war into the back yards of his enemies by heading north. He planned to destroy the railroad bridge at Harrisburg, Pennsylvania, and then turn his attention to Philadelphia, Baltimore, or Washington. After the long march north, Confederate troops were spread from Chambersburg, through Carlisle, and into York. Thousands of soldiers passed through dozens of towns and hamlets in southern Pennsylvania, where they searched for much needed supplies that would enable them to continue the Southern offensive.

In July of 1863, Lee's Army of Northern Virginia of seventy four thousand men and the ninety eight thousand man Union Army of the Potomac met, by chance, when a Confederate brigade was sent forward to intercept a shipment of badly needed shoes near Gettysburg, Pennsylvania. By the summer of 1863, it was estimated that less than forty percent of the Confederate Army had shoes. Little did these men know that the events that were about to occur on that day would forever change their lives and American history.

The most decisive battle of the war began as an accidental encounter in the village of Gettysburg on July 1. A Federal general observed a portion of Lee's army moving into Gettysburg along the Chambersburg Turnpike. At three thirty that afternoon, the order came to attack. The only Georgia brigade in the early battle was the one that included Captain Yopp, Bill, and the boys of the 14th. The battle climaxed with the storming of Seminary Ridge. Bill's company was in the middle of the worst fighting. As the brutal afternoon continued, Bill's brigade was positioned in reserve to protect the artillery from a threatened enemy advance on the left flank.

At five o'clock Lee asked his generals to launch an attack on the Union forces that were loosely entrenched on Cemetery Ridge, which lay one mile to the east across a broad open valley. Much of it was planted in waist–high wheat. With support divisions being too distant to the rear and his men being tired and nearly out of ammunition, Lee decided to wait until the next day to attack.

Lee's greatest opportunity to take the ridge was lost when the Federals dug in during the night.

Bill and the men in his company were positioned south of the Gettysburg Seminary, along Seminary Ridge and the Chambersburg Road in support of the artillery. From this point, they would witness the bloody suicidal attacks on Cemetery Ridge on the second and third days. During the night, the brigade moved off the ridge, about a half–mile toward Cemetery Ridge. There, in a ravine, they were exposed to Federal sharpshooters and a hot July sun. The 14th Regiment formed the left flank of the brigade, and they had avoided most of the fighting. In spite of their lack of major action, they were not sent to Pickett and Pettigrew's aid during their fateful charge up Cemetery Ridge.

The assault consisted of forty–one regiments with four brigades held in reserve. Pickett and Pettigrew's men, totaling over fifteen thousand, were slaughtered by harrowing, close quarter cannon fire and the blasts of fifty thousand Union muskets as they crossed the expansive open field. Many speculated that if the four reserve brigades had been brought to the front, Pickett might have breached the wall.

The attack was so devastating that Lee retreated to Virginia and did not conduct any major engagements until the following spring. With the failure of Pickett's Charge, the battle was over. The Union was saved. Lee's retreat began on the afternoon of July 4. Behind him, this small town of only 2,400 was left with over fifty one thousand casualties. Over one hundred and seventy thousand men and six hundred cannons had been positioned in an area encompassing twenty–five square miles. Additionally, an estimated five hundred and fifty tons of ammunition had been expended. When the battle had ended, five thousand dead horses and the other wreckage of war presented a scene of terrible devastation.

The Confederate army that staggered back from the fight at Gettysburg was physically and spiritually exhausted. Lee would never again attempt an offensive operation of such proportions. Union General Meade, though criticized for not immediately pursuing Lee's army, carried the day in the battle that has become known as the High Water Mark of the Confederacy.

The Battle of Gettysburg was also a major turning point in the life of Captain Thomas Yopp and his lifelong relationship with Bill. It all began during Picket's Charge. As the advancing soldiers marched past the men of the 14th Regiment, a commander of the reserve Confederate brigade became enraged that he would not get to participate in the glorious attack.

"Sitting in the rear is for the wounded and sickly, not for my strong boys from Georgia," he was heard saying.

Contrary to direct orders, in a moment of weakness, he ordered his men to join Pickett and attack. At that late point in the battle, it was obvious to everyone in the field that the massive attack was futile. Virtually all of the junior and senior Confederate officers of the brigade began pleading with their commanders to reconsider.

Finally, out of sheer frustration and with no concern for his own fate, Captain Yopp raced to his commander and flatly refused to order his men forward to their certain deaths. Upon doing this, he was immediately relieved of his command.

General Lee, who had ordered the brigade to wait in reserve, became furious that his commanders had ignored his orders. He demanded that the brigade halt its advance and return to the reserve position to protect their flank. It appeared that Captain Yopp's actions would be forgiven, but, for whatever reasons, the distraught commander maintained the charges of insubordination against Captain Yopp. He had Yopp cashiered, or demoted, to the rank of private. His glorious career as an army officer was finished. In spite of this blow, Thomas Yopp remained a very proud man who knew he had saved the lives of countless fellow Georgians by refusing to send them into the whirlwind of certain death. After serving with Bill and the other men of the company through the fall and winter of 1863–64 as a private, Thomas requested and received a transfer to report to the Confederate Navy on board the side–wheel ship *Patrick Henry* on April 2, 1864. The *Patrick Henry* was modified earlier in the war from a battle cruiser to a school ship and housed the Confederate States' Naval Academy on the James River where Thomas served. When Richmond was razed by the Yankees on April 3, 1865, the *Patrick Henry* was burned to prevent its capture. Bill was not allowed to join Thomas and was devastated that he had left the unit, but

Bill remained loyal to the men from Georgia throughout the final months of the war.

Following Thomas' departure from Company H, the war raged for an additional twelve terrible and tormenting months. The Confederacy and Bill Yopp never recovered from the losses at Gettysburg. Through the deepening twilight of Confederate military might, all who had been at Gettysburg would never forget its horror.

Bill was present with his regiment when General Lee surrendered at Appomattox Court House on April 9, 1865. The official surrender at Appomattox recorded thirteen tired and sickly soldiers listed on the rolls of Company H, a far cry from the boisterous 130 men who left Laurens County in July 1861, ready for a fight.

By that time, Bill had become an indispensable member of his company Time after time he had shown uncommon bravery and compassion as he rushed onto the battlefields to rescue friends or to pour cool water on the parched and bloody lips of a dying soldier. He had cared for the sick and wounded, fed the hungry, written letters home for his friends, told grief–stricken wives of the loss of their husbands, and offered a sympathetic ear when the boys wanted to talk or cry. No matter how busy or tired Bill was, he always had time to aid a friend in need and rarely asked for favors in return.

Bill Yopp celebrated his twentieth birthday shortly after the final shots of the Civil War were fired.

THE BEGINNING OF
A NEW DAY

When the surrender was complete, Bill and the small group of haggard survivors from Laurens County turned south and slowly began making the five hundred mile trek home. The long days of walking and searching for food seemed unending. The excitement over the war's end soon wore off as the men trudged mile after mile down the dusty roads of Virginia, North Carolina, and South Carolina. They walked side by side with hundreds of ragged and filthy Confederate soldiers who were bound for hundreds of farms and small towns throughout the south.

They came over a hill on a long straight road while walking through South Carolina early one morning. As far as they could see, there were small groups of soldiers struggling toward their families and their homes. Dirty and hungry men covered the landscape like a plague of locusts, eating whatever they could find and sleeping wherever there was shelter. Large and small towns alike were forced to open soup kitchens for the starving soldiers and invite them into their churches for rest. Small town doctors were overrun with soldiers requiring medical attention for their illnesses or war injuries. None of these men had any money.

As the weary soldiers drew closer to Georgia, they began hearing more stories about the burning of Atlanta and the destruction caused by Union General Sherman during his march to the sea seven months earlier. However, no descriptions could prepare them for the true awfulness of the devastation they were about to find. The once majestic city of Atlanta had been reduced to piles of rubble, and burned out skeletons of huge homes dotted the scene. The once tree–filled landscape was barren and smoke–filled. Thousands of women, children, and elderly citizens were given two days to pack their belongings and leave the city to fend for themselves on the back roads of Georgia.

On November 12, 1864, Sherman marched out of Atlanta toward the Atlantic coast. When he completed his task, the area between Atlanta and Savannah looked like a huge, fiery scythe had carved a swath of destruction over sixty miles wide and two hundred miles long. No other campaign in the war contributed more to keeping alive sectional animosity than Sherman's march through Georgia and South Carolina.

The march began shortly after the fall crops had been harvested, so the Union army found the barns bursting with grain, fodder, and peas. The warehouses were full of cotton. Yards were crowded with hogs, chickens, and turkeys. The soldiers in the southern armies were starving, not because there was no food, but because the railroads had been destroyed. It became impossible to send supplies to the front. Sherman was not content with simply using what food and supplies he needed. He boasted that he would "smash things to the sea and make Georgia howl." His men entered homes, taking everything of value that could be moved. They also slaughtered thousands of hogs, sheep, and poultry as they stood in the pen.

Many homes were burned without any justification, especially the mansions of the former slave owners. Sherman testified to the conduct of his men in his memoirs, estimating that he had destroyed $80 million worth of property, of which he could make no use. He described it as "simple waste and destruction." One of the most serious aspects of his work was the destruction of the railroads; the Central of Georgia from Macon to Savannah was almost totally ruined.

—

As Bill and the small band of ragged soldiers walked into the outskirts of Dublin on May 6, a wagon train containing a dozen large covered wagons rumbled through the streets and stopped in the middle of town. The large wagons and teams kicked up such a thick cloud of dust that it was five minutes before anyone could see what was happening. The sound of the wagons and teams was deafening. People scrambled from all corners of the small town to see who and what this could be. A wagon train of this size was an uncommon sight in Laurens County in 1865. Word spread quickly that the wagons held the retreating president of the Confederacy, Jefferson Davis, and his cabinet.

When the defense of the Confederate capital became impossible on the night of April 2, 1865 the Confederate government had evacuated Richmond. In the following weeks, the surrender of Confederate armies in Virginia and North Carolina forced Jefferson Davis and his government to retreat even farther south. Davis' plan was to retreat to Florida, where a ship would be waiting to take him to Mexico.

Bill and several of his friends, still wearing what was left of their tattered Confederate uniforms, stood on the walkway outside of F.H. Rowe's General Store and witnessed this grand site. Bill mentioned in later years that he saw Davis as he climbed from a wagon and began greeting many of the citizens of Dublin. The entourage, comprised of Davis' cabinet members and soldiers, set up camp near the Oconee River bridge and stayed there on May 6 and 7 before continuing their fateful journey south. It was at this site where Jefferson Davis was reunited with his wife and children, who had made the long journey from Richmond in a separate wagon train using a different route south.

Several days later, on May 10, Jefferson Davis was captured in the small town of Irwinville, Georgia, thus ending the hopes of any reprisals against the Union. He was charged with treason and imprisoned for two years before being released.

As long as Bill lived, he loved to tell the story about standing on the steps of Rowe's Store and seeing President

Jefferson Davis. It was the first true dignitary he ever saw, but it would not be the last.

Following Bill's remarkable chance encounter with President Davis, he said his sad goodbyes to his fellow army friends and began walking to Whitehall. He had heard from a man in Dublin that Thomas had come home two weeks earlier. He was especially anxious to see him and find out everything he had been doing since they last saw each other over a year earlier.

—

When he turned onto the main road at Whitehall, Bill knew immediately that things had changed since he had last been home. He stopped on the lane, scanned everything in sight, and then moved on. The huge cotton fields grew tall with weeds and brush. It looked as if no crops had been grown in them for years. As he drew closer to the big house, he noticed a large vegetable garden had been planted in the back yard of the home, where once Miss Margaret had grown a rose garden. What was left of her formal flower gardens was unkempt. The paint was peeling from the house. One of the shutters hung sideways off its hinge and gave the impression that no one had cared for the place in years.

It did not seem like over two years had passed since he last walked up the front steps of the Yopp house, yet he could sense that much had changed. After a few raps on the front door, he heard footsteps and saw someone move in front of the window toward the door. When the big door opened, Bill was greeted by Thomas. Both men broke into huge grins. They immediately stepped forward, vigorously shook each other's hand, and slapped each other on the back.

"Bill, you finally made it home," Thomas exclaimed. He stepped back to look at his long time friend. "We have all been wondering when you would get here. It's wonderful to have you back."

"Masr, it is so nice to see you and be home," Bill said as he removed his cap and held it to his chest. "I been worryin' about you for months. I didn't know where you were."

Thomas shook his head apologetically, smiled, and replied, "I do appreciate your letters, Bill. I found it most enjoyable to be able to keep up with the comings and goings of the unit. We had little news worth mentioning where I was, so I was a poor writer."

"We better get you in here so everyone can see you," Thomas said, welcoming Bill through the front door. "There have been lots of changes around here since you were last home, and we need to tell you all the news."

From the tone of Thomas' voice, Bill could tell that the changes had not been for the better.

—

The next few days were a wonderful reunion for Bill and the people of Whitehall Plantation. William and Lia hovered over Bill like mother hens over their chicks and pampered him constantly. He learned that Jeremiah had called all of the slaves together earlier in the year and had given each of them a signed letter that verified they were now free men. Since none of them could read, they lined up for him to read each letter to its recipient. Several of them asked him to read the letter twice, just so they could fully understand and appreciate what was happening. Over the course of the following weeks, many of the slaves had chosen to leave the farm in an effort to find paying jobs in Dublin or other cities. The remainder of the former slaves, mostly the older families, had elected to stay on the farm as tenant farmers. They paid rent to Jeremiah Yopp with any money they could earn from their small piece of land.

Since the cotton and tobacco markets were almost nonexistent, the Yopps were essentially bankrupt. They were soon relying upon the goodwill of their former slaves for their sustenance. Each Saturday afternoon the black families on the farm would leave vegetables or wild game at the big house for the Yopps so they could survive. The once proud Jeremiah Yopp became so distraught over their predicament that he closed himself in the library in the big house and came out only a few times a day. In spite of the pleadings of Miss Margaret and Thomas, Jeremiah refused to accept the fact that his once great estate and wonderful life were in ruins.

Bill had no choice but to try his hand at farming since there were no more jobs for him at the big house. His parents and two sisters remained with the Yopps as their cook and house servants, but the other children were on their own. Sometime before 1870, Bill married a girl of the same age named Anna. They lived next door to his father and mother in a small shanty. No records have been found showing that they had any children. Bill worked hard for five years and barely scraped out a living. He even found himself running a liquor still with his brother for several years, trying to make enough money to get by. Bill found little joy in the pitiful existence that the once proud plantation had enjoyed. He longed for his childhood days of laughter, singing, hunting, and fishing with Thomas, but things were different now. Life at Whitehall held little joy for anyone.

—

In the spring of 1866, Miss Margaret walked into the library one morning to find that Jeremiah had died while sitting at his desk. It was another blow in what seemed like an unending string of sorrowful events to hit the family. Bill would later say that those years on the plantation were some of the unhappiest years of his life. Thomas stayed so busy trying to manage the farm and make enough money for the survival of his family that he hardly had time for his old friend.

Finally, in late 1870, Bill had had enough and decided to leave the farm for the big city. It is not known if his wife, Anna, passed away or whether they were divorced, but the last record of her was in the 1870 census with Bill. Whatever the case, Bill yearned for a life of adventure and travel. He knew that he had to give it a try while he was still young. Thomas and Miss Margaret wrote glowing letters of recommendation for him as they sent him on his way, riding a horse that Thomas had given him.

With twenty dollars in his pocket, a clean suit, and an old horse, Bill set out to make his mark on the world. It was the beginning of a new day in his life, and he intended to make the best of it.

THERE AIN'T NO BETTER MEDICINE THAN A GOOD DOSE OF FAMILY

OCTOBER 1870

The old sway–backed horse sauntered steadily north toward the city of Macon, while Bill enjoyed the autumn countryside and sang his favorite songs. The cool October air was a refreshing break from the hot sultry days he had lived through on the farm. It was refreshing to know that once again he was starting a new journey. He passed a number of wagons, riders, and walkers, and always tipped his hat and wished them a good day. Bill, now twenty–five years old, contemplated what kind of job he would try to find when he arrived in Macon, a bustling city only one hundred miles south of Atlanta. Something Thomas had told him shortly before his departure continued to ring through his head.

"Bill, if you are going to make a good living, you should find out where the wealthy people spend their time and get a job there," Thomas had said in a fatherly tone. "Not only will you be more likely to make good money in a place such as that, but you'll see how they make their money and perhaps one day get your chance to do the same."

Thomas had made several suggestions, and one

of those was that he try to get a job at the biggest and grandest hotel in Macon, The Brown House Hotel. The old Victorian hotel that sat across the street from the bustling railroad station was a true landmark. It was also the place where wealthy and powerful businessmen and politicians gathered when they were in town. Bill reached into his jacket pocket and removed the torn newspaper advertisement that Thomas had given to him. He read it again.

THE BROWN HOUSE—Opposite the Passenger Depot in downtown Macon. George B. Welsh, Hotel Manager. Very convenient and an excellent house. Visitors can take off their boots when they go to bed with the assurance that they will not be stolen by servants who carry the pass-keys. In case such a thing should happen, the gentlemanly landlord would afford ample satisfaction. At the other house it is positively necessary to go to bed with your boots on if you do not wish to be put to the trouble of going out the next morning in your stockings to buy a new pair.

Upon arrival in the busy city of Macon, Bill went directly to the hotel and inquired with the desk clerk about possible employment. He made certain the clerk knew that he had letters of recommendation from upstanding citizens of Laurens County. Minutes later he was escorted into a large office and introduced to George Welsh, the hotel manager.

The middle–aged manager had a pleasant smile, short gray hair, and a plump belly, which was the result of sampling too many of the savory pies cooked in his kitchen. He wore a tight pair of wire–rimmed glasses and squinted over the top of them when he spoke. After telling Bill to take a seat in a big chair opposite his desk, he took a few minutes to read the letters from Thomas and Miss Margaret. When he finished the second letter, the good natured manager looked up at Bill and began asking questions.

"Bill," he said, "I remember your old master, Jeremiah Yopp. He stayed here several times." He glanced back down at the letters. "These are certainly glowing letters that make you appear to be a perfect fit for employment in our hotel. Have you ever had any experience working in the hotel business?"

Pushing out to the edge of his seat, Bill smiled and nervously replied, "Mr. Welsh, suh, I have spent my entire life helping take care of my Masr and his family. All during the war I took care of a whole company of men. I feel like I probably have more experience at taking care of other folks than most people ever get." He paused. "You might say that I was born to look after folks and make them feel at home. And Mr. Welsh, I can tell you that I am an honest man down to the bone, and I don't have any laziness in my body at all."

Welsh had taken an immediate liking to Bill and grinned when he completed his comments.

"Bill, I do feel that you will fit in well here. I'd like for you to meet Mr. Brown, the owner of our hotel. If he feels the same as I do, then we will offer you a job. He will be in within the hour if you don't mind waiting to see him," Welsh said as he stood up from his desk.

—

Mr. E.E. Brown was the long time owner of the hotel, having opened it on January 1, 1856. He had built a solid reputation that spread far and wide for having one of the most pleasant hotel and restaurant establishments in the state of Georgia. The balding, elderly man was approaching eighty years old and had been in poor health, but he still came to work almost daily and helped his manager meet and greet the guests. He was a stickler for exuding hospitality to everyone. He was also a kind and generous man who was well respected within the state and local community. Mr. Brown and his wife moved into a large room at the hotel so that they could be closer to their business and their guests. The Brown House Hotel was now their home, and the employees and guests were their family.

Shortly after Bill's successful meeting with Mr. Brown, he began his first job as a bellboy, working the busy front door and lobby of the hotel. His job was to greet the guests, carry their luggage to their rooms, hail carriages, and help the travelers with any questions or problems they might have.

Mr. Welsh told Bill about an inexpensive boarding house down the street where several black employees lived and he could rent a room. Then he gave Bill his new blue bellboy's suit, shiny black shoes that actually fit, white cotton gloves, and a red felt top hat. Bill was so proud of his new wardrobe that he wore it for two hours in his room that night and practiced what he would say when he greeted hotel guests.

As had been the case with Bill's life up to this point, it took only a short while for him to become an indispens-able employee and friend to the management, staff, and regular clientele of the hotel. One of his most notable assets was his ability to remember the names of the guests and their preferences

After less than two years on the job, the elite and powerful of the state knew Bill well. They always enjoyed being greeted and served by him when they came to the hotel. The governor, congressmen, senators, mayors, and even a few foreign dignitaries graced the hotel, and Bill's reputation for friendliness and service became known by each of them. Everyone was impressed with how Bill could remember not only the names of the dignitaries, but their wives, children, and pets who occasionally accompa-nied them. He knew their favorite meals and their brand of liquor. He always had a big cigar on a silver tray for the men who smoked. He knew how to make these people feel special, yet he maintained an air of dignity, poise, and benevolence that was a rare and prized trait. On several occasions, some of the more powerful politicians even asked Bill what the secret was to his exceptional memory. Bill always gave the same response.

He would rub his chin in a thoughtful pose and then say, "Well, you know, suh, I forgot."

With that said, everyone would burst into laughter. Even that became a memorable part of Bill's personality. Returning guests would call out to him, "Bill, have you remembered why you have such a good memory?" He would reply, "No, suh, still workin' on that."

Bill searched for ways to ingratiate himself with the management and clientele of the hotel because it gave him so much satisfaction to please other people. Whenever important guests traveled with their children, Bill always went out of his way to make the little ones feel welcome, too. One day, when the wife of a businessman became ill, Bill took their two young daughters on a carriage ride around the city while the doctor cared for their mother. Bill always kept a pocket full of candy and a few magic tricks ready for all of the children. The attention never went unnoticed, and Bill's reputation as a loving and caring man continued to grow. As a result of Bill's hard work and dedication, Mr. Brown promoted him to the position of front manager and placed him in charge of all bellboys. He was always sought out to plan menus for important returning guests. Bill thrived on the added responsibility and respect that came with his new title.

As the months passed, the elderly hotel owner and

Bill became very good friends. Each day at 3:00 p.m., Bill would carry a pot of herbal tea and some fresh cookies to the old man's room. He would sit down with him and talk about anything that came up. On some days, Mr. Brown would talk of his early years when he and his young family moved to Macon and opened the hotel. Bill reminisced with him about life on the plantation and some of the tales from his days during the war. Mr. Brown found it all very fascinating and could never get enough of Bill's adventurous life story. Gradually their long conversations created a bond of friendship between the two men.

Bill had been working at the hotel for a little over two years when Mr. Brown's health took a turn for the worse. His doctors and family determined that he should go to Connecticut, where he could escape the heat and humidity of the south. and be cared for by his younger brother's family. One afternoon Brown sent word that he would like to visit with Bill in his room. A few minutes later, Bill knocked softly on the door to announce his presence and entered the room. The elderly man was sitting in his favorite rocking chair, facing the window, when Bill joined him.

"Afternoon, Mr. Brown," Bill said with a slight bow as he entered the dimly lit room. "How are you feeling today, suh?"

"I'm no spring chicken anymore, Bill, but thank you for asking," Mr. Brown said with a shaky voice. "Bill, the reason I called you up here is to ask you to do a favor for me. I don't know if anyone has told you that the doctors feel I should go to Hartford, Connecticut for my health. They think I'll feel better up there."

True concern was written on Bill's smooth young face.

"I'm very sorry to hear about that, Mr. Brown, but I'm sure those doctors know what is best for you. I hate the thought that you won't be around here every day to tell me your latest jokes," Bill said. He grinned after his attempt at humor with the elderly man. He paused for a moment. "And what is it that you would like for me to do for you, suh? You know that I'll do anything in the world for you, Mr. Brown," Bill said sincerely as he stood in front of the old man holding his red hat in his white gloved hands.

"Bill," Mr. Brown said as he turned and looked out the window, "I'd like to hire you to help me make the trip to Connecticut. I will pay all of your expenses, plus pay you a salary to escort me."

Without any thought, Bill knew immediately that this was an adventure that he wanted to take. He wasn't sure where Connecticut was, but the thought of a new journey made his pulse quicken.

"Will I still have my job here at the hotel when I return?" Bill asked.

"Certainly, Bill," Brown said. He grinned. "I think you'll probably be running this place one of these years, if the guests keep complimenting you the way they have up to now."

Bill smiled broadly and replied, "I'd be honored to

help you out, Mr. Brown. Jes tell me when you want to leave, and I'll be here to help you."

The old man smiled and held out his frail hand to shake Bill's. "That's wonderful, Bill. We'll have a grand trip together. We will take the train to Savannah, go by passenger steamer to New York, and then on up to New Haven. My friends will meet us at the port there, and then you can return home on the next southbound steamer. I can assure you that you will enjoy the trip," he said. "And while we are traveling together, I think we'll finally have the time for you to tell me more of the wonderful stories about your experiences during the war."

Just like that, the world of travel had opened up to Bill Yopp. Bill had no idea that this would become just the first of his many excursions around the United States and the world…an amazing accomplishment for this former slave from the cotton fields of Georgia.

Bill soon discovered that every day of traveling with Mr. Brown brought new sights and experiences that kept a perpetual smile on his face. His first ride on a modern passenger train was an unexpected pleasure.

After getting Mr. Brown situated in the first class car, Bill took a window seat with the other black travelers who rode in the rear car. All he could think of as he boarded the train for the five–hour ride to Savannah was the time he rode on the roof of a boxcar with Thomas. Despite the horrors that followed those earlier train rides, his mind revisited only the fond memories of those days.

Not long after the train left Macon, Bill walked to the

rear of the last car and stepped onto the open deck. Over an hour had gone by when one of his new acquaintances, a fellow named Jim, realized that Bill had not returned to his seat. He went to the rear, searching for him. "I think I seen Bill climb up that ladder to the roof a while back," a black woman in her forties told Jim. He walked quickly to the rear door. Panic spread on his face when he opened the door only to find an empty deck. Remembering what the woman had told him, he quickly climbed the metal ladder to the roof. Upon peering over the top, he spotted Bill sitting cross–legged and staring peacefully off at the green countryside.

"What you doing up here on the roof, Bill?" Jim called out over the clatter of the train.

Bill turned and smiled. He said, "Jes up here getting some fresh air. I'm remembering my days during the war and all the good friends I had. We had some mighty fine times up here."

"You better come back down or you goin' to get blown off of here," Jim pleaded.

Bill sat silently and didn't hear a thing Jim had said. A tear rolled down his cheek and quickly dried in the breeze. If you had seen it, you would not have known whether the tear was caused by sorrow or simply the rush of the wind. A beaming smile crossed his face as he turned and looked down the roofline of the long, snaking train. He remembered the hundreds of miles he and Thomas had ridden up here together. He missed his old friend and wished Thomas was here with him.

—

Upon arrival in Savannah, their luggage was loaded onto a wagon. He and Mr. Brown made their way to the busy docks on the Savannah River, where they boarded their side–wheel steamship for Connecticut. Bill had never seen anything but drawings or paintings of ships; he had never laid eyes on the ocean and had no idea what lay ahead. When the loud steam whistle blasted its departure announcement, Bill nearly jumped out of his skin. He had not heard anything that loud since the cannon fire of the war.

As the huge paddle wheels slowly began pulling through the black water, a certain sense of fear of the unknown raced through his mind. He quickly overcame it, though, as he became captivated by the blue, borderless ocean. The beauty and scope of the sea was mesmerizing, and the thought of plowing along on a side–wheeler excited him beyond anything he had ever experienced. He could hardly wait for sunrise each morning so that he could rush onto the deck to gaze at the new vistas, breathe in the clean salt air, and study the odd fish that swam up to inspect the noisy ship. He grew especially fond of standing on the bow and watching the playful dolphins skim through the waves, performing their acrobatics for their fascinated audience. Mr. Brown got great enjoyment from watching Bill's reaction to these new experiences, almost like a father watching his child make new discoveries.

—

The wonderful days at sea passed by much too quickly for Bill. Soon the ship was docking for the night in New York harbor. Mr. Brown had tried to prepare Bill for what lay ahead, but no quantity of words could adequately describe the largest city in America. As far as Bill could see in every direction, there were buildings of all shapes and sizes, large groups of busy people scurrying along the streets and docks, colorful flags waving in the wind, and dozens upon dozens of ships and boats of all sizes tied to the docks. Large three–mast schooners drifted silently through the harbor, while noisy steam engines and horns pierced the late afternoon air. Boisterous workers pushed huge wagonloads of fish along the docks. Thick flocks of sea gulls floated, screamed, and dived like flies over spilled honey. Odd–looking people from foreign lands, wearing clothes unlike anything he had ever seen, strolled in small groups along the docks and chattered away in peculiar tongues. Bill stood on the deck for hours, captivated by it all.

With a fresh group of passengers aboard and crates of freight loaded during the night, the ship set sail at sunrise the next day for the trip to the busy seaport of New Haven. Standing on the chilly early morning deck with Bill, Mr. Brown suddenly grew quite serious and turned to speak.

"Bill," Mr. Brown began. He reached over and placed his gloved hand affectionately on Bill's arm. "I wanted to thank you again for being such a good friend and companion to me over the past two years. You have brought me much happiness, and I will truly miss seeing you each day."

Bill smiled and shook his head from side to side.

"Mr. Brown, suh, you don't need to be thanking me for none of that. It has been my pleasure to spend time with you. You are one of the nicest people I have ever met, and I know you are going to be feeling much better once you get settled in up here with your family. Ain't no better medicine for what ails you than a good dose of family."

"Well, I certainly appreciate that," Brown said. He grinned at Bill's comment and looked out over the ocean. "I also wanted to tell you that if you ever decide you would like to come back up this way, I will do everything in my power to help you get a good job. I have written a letter for you that should help you with introductions," he said as he reached into his inside jacket pocket. He removed an envelope and gave it to Bill. "Please write me and let me know what you are doing. Do not hesitate to ask for my help if there is anything that you need."

Bill was moved to tears by the kindness and sincerity of Mr. Brown. Pools of water filled his eyes, and a knot of emotion choked his throat.

"I don't know quite what to say, Mr. Brown," he said as he wiped a tear from his cheek with the back of his hand. "I will always remember you, and hopefully one day soon I can get back up here to see you. You are mighty kind to offer to help me."

—

Bill stared out across the misty early morning waters of the Atlantic and took a deep breath of the invigorating, crisp salt air. He pulled his jacket collar closer around his neck and closed his eyes. He felt the energy that is only produced by welcome change and new opportunities, and he liked what he felt. He knew deep inside that his life had been changed forever by the kind old man and his experiences in the last few weeks.

He also knew that one day he would be returning to the sea.

THE ONLY WAY TO HAVE A FRIEND IS TO BE ONE

JULY 1873

As wonderful as working at the Macon hotel had been for Bill, life there would never be the same after his adventure to Connecticut. Despite coming home to the warm and friendly hotel and rejoining his many friends, he soon had strong feelings that life held more for him than opening doors and carrying luggage in a steamy, middle Georgia town. His wandering spirit beckoned for change, so in July of 1873, Bill walked into Mr. Welsh's office and apologetically tendered his resignation.

Losing Bill was a crushing blow to Welsh and the Brown family, who felt strongly that one of the greatest assets of the hotel was Bill's reputation with their clients. His service and hospitality had truly differentiated The Brown House from all other hotels in Macon and possibly the entire state of Georgia. Aside from his hard work and pleasant demeanor, he had made countless suggestions to Mr. Welsh for the improvement of service to the guests. The changes were always well received by the guests, and Bill was always given credit for his efforts. After trying everything he could think of to convince Bill to stay, Mr. Welsh soon realized that money and comfort had little to do with Bill's reasons for leaving.

Bill stayed at the hotel for several more weeks to train his replacement and pack his belongings at the boarding house. He thought it was odd when Mr. Welsh told him to take his last busy Saturday afternoon off as a paid holiday, but he didn't argue and thoroughly enjoyed the free time. Around eight o'clock that evening, the young man whom Bill had been training came to his room and said, "Something has come up. Mr. Welsh needs you back over at the hotel in about thirty minutes." This too was puzzling, but the young man offered no further explanation. Bill quickly put on his suit, thinking that Mr. Welsh needed him to work some unexpected function.

Upon entering the front door of the hotel, the young bellboy told Bill that Mr. Welsh was in the dining room. As the huge sliding doors to the dining room slid open, a great roar went up from over fifty people who had gathered for a surprise celebration in Bill's honor. Most were dressed in their evening clothes as if they were going to a night at the opera. Horns blew, music played, and cheers went up throughout the grand Victorian room. A large paper banner hung from a wall that read, "Best of Luck, Bill. We will all miss you." Bill's eyes opened widely and his jaw dropped in total surprise as he quickly recognized the familiar faces of big businessmen, local politicians, and dozens of regular hotel clients. Each of them had been personally invited by Mr. Welsh to join them for his farewell salute. Bill was dumbfounded. He could not believe that so many important people had gathered to wish him well. Bill kept saying, "Y'all done all of this for me?"

Welsh awkwardly climbed up onto a chair and clinked a wine glass with a butter knife to get everyone's attention. When the noise diminished, Mr. Welsh began speaking as he peered over his reading glasses.

"Ladies, gentlemen, and our guest of honor, Bill Yopp," he said loudly, flashing his big, contagious smile. "I want to thank each of you for taking the time out of your busy schedules to join us tonight. We are here to honor our good friend, Bill Yopp, who has made the unpopular decision to leave Macon so that he can travel and see the world. While we can't bear the thought of him leaving our fair city, we do want to let him know how much we appreciate what he has done for us and that he will truly be missed by the hotel and each of you." Welsh then paused and turned to face Bill. "Everyone in this room will miss your smiling face, your kindness, and your unselfishness. We wish you the best of everything. Good things come to good people, and you have certainly earned the admiration and praise of everyone in this room. We hope you will keep in touch with us and that one day soon you will return to Macon to see all of your old friends and share your memories from your adventures."

Welsh reached down to the table, picked up a glass of champagne, and gave it to Bill. He then raised his glass toward Bill and said, "Here is a toast to you, Bill. Best of luck." A rumble of "bravos" came from the assembled guests, whom all tipped their glasses and toasted Bill.

Loud applause broke out from the group. Everyone smiled broadly and looked straight at Bill. They moved into a large circle around him so they could all see his face. Tears filled Bill's eyes, and he looked down at the floor to gather his thoughts. The applause went on for what seemed like forever. Finally the short black man held up his right hand, smiled, and tried to speak. As he did, the crowd grew silent.

"I hope you'll understand when I don't drink my champagne. The last time any alcohol touched my lips was right before the war, and I just recently recuperated from that swig," he said with a smile. The group roared with laughter.

As the hilarity died down, Bill's face became more serious.

"When I was a little boy, my daddy told me one day that the only way to have a friend is to be one. It took me a few years to understand exactly what he was talking about, but I finally learned that you got to work at being a good friend. And this is exactly what each of you are doing tonight; you are working at being my friends. I can't think of any words that can tell you how much I appreciate what you have done for me during my years here at the hotel.

"These past few years at The Brown House have been some of the best of my life. I have enjoyed getting to know each one of you and your families. I'll be leaving here tomorrow and don't rightly know where I'll end up, but that's a big part of the reason why I'm leaving. The fact that I can just pack up my suitcase and move on to another city, another job, or even to another country is something that none of my folks have ever been able to do. If the President of these United States says I am a free man, then I plan to go places and see things that I can talk about when I am an old man sitting under a tree, telling tales to some wide eyed chillun'. And one thing I know for sure," he said before pausing to look around at all of the smiling faces, "I'll always tell those chillun' about the fine folks in Macon, Georgia. I will never forget you."

The party went on into the late hours that night, as everyone wanted to shake hands with Bill, proclaim their appreciation for his past kindnesses, and offer to help him with any endeavors he might have in the future. Throughout the evening men were walking up to Bill and giving him envelopes that contained letters of glowing recommendation for the job he had done at The Brown House. Several people presented him with beautifully wrapped gift boxes that contained items such as new socks, neckties, tie tacks, and cuff links. He was so moved by the overwhelming show of appreciation that he found himself standing there speechless while everyone carried on around him.

It was approaching eleven o'clock when Mr. Welsh once again tapped on a glass to get everyone's attention. When the group had quieted, he spoke.

"Bill, us old–timers need to call it a night and get some rest. But before we go, I have a special gift for you that was sent by Mr. E.E. Brown up in Hartford."

With that said Welsh held out a small wrapped box and presented it to Bill.

"Please open it, Bill," Welsh said.

The crowd of men and women hushed as everyone pushed closer to see what gift the wealthy Mr. Brown had sent him. Bill took the small box in his hand, carefully removed the shiny paper and lace bow, and opened the top. After lifting out some cotton, Bill could clearly see the gleaming gold ink pen with his name, "Bill Yopp," fancily engraved on it. Once again, he held his breath in shock as he gingerly lifted the exquisite pen from the box and held it up for everyone to see. The room filled with oohs and aahs and some scattered applause. In the bottom of the box was a small card with handwriting that Bill recognized as Mr. Brown's. When the group saw him remove the card, several people asked that he read it out loud.

In a shaky, emotion–filled voice, Bill read the card. "To Bill Yopp, who has crossed more hurdles than most and shown more heart than any. May the oceans you sail and the roads you travel be smooth and friendly, and may this pen one day write the story of your wonderful life." It was signed, "Your friend, E.E. Brown."

When all of the guests left the big dining room that night, Bill remained behind to savor one of the greatest moments of his life. Sitting alone at a table with only one flickering gaslight left on in the quiet room, he wiped more tears from his eyes and stared at the beautiful pen. No one in his family had ever owned anything so beautiful. He would keep it as one of his prized possessions for the remainder of his life.

—

As the flickering light threw dancing shadows across the ceiling and walls of the big room, Bill contemplated his decision to leave Macon. He hoped he had made the right choice to move on. *Only time would tell,* he thought. *Only time would tell.*

I'VE COME TO TAKE
YOU HOME

AUGUST 1873

Bill excitedly returned to Whitehall to visit his friends and family and plan his next adventure. Thomas was especially pleased to see Bill, and they soon planned several days of hunting and fishing together, just like old times. They packed up a wagon and headed down to their favorite spot on the river where they pitched a camp and stayed for three glorious days and nights. The fish were biting, and Bill's cooking was even better than Thomas had remembered. Their first night sitting by the campfire brought back a flood of fond memories and sad reflections from the last time they had camped together in Virginia.

Bill's mother celebrated her birthday while he was there. He presented her with a new store–bought dress and a colorful hat covered with ribbons, which were soon the envy of all the church ladies. He brought his father a new pair of shoes, which were the first new pair he had ever owned. Bill spent hours upon hours sitting under the spreading oaks with his family and friends, telling them about his life in Macon and the wonderful trip he took to Connecticut. His descriptions of the train ride and the days on the steamship mesmerized everyone.

While Bill's life had been exciting, fulfilling, and productive, life at Whitehall had continued to spiral downward with the worsening economy of the postwar South. The once wealthy agricultural region was paralyzed from poor markets for their products and a general lack of available labor and cash on the once huge plantations. Carpetbaggers from the north had swept into the area with pockets full of cash and taken advantage of every poor landowner who was strapped for money. It seemed to Thomas that a different family on the farm packed up their sparse belongings and departed for the bigger cities in the hope for better lives almost monthly. At its peak in 1861, the once bustling plantation had over forty people living and working on it. In the summer of 1873, fewer than a dozen people lived there.

It was no surprise to anyone when Bill announced at dinner one night that he would be leaving the next day. He had made up his mind to travel to Savannah to see what kind of work he could find in that bustling city. After another sad morning of farewells, Thomas volunteered to take Bill into Dublin so that he could catch the train to the coast.

Standing at the train depot, Thomas smiled and held out his hand to Bill. He said, "Well, old friend, it has been mighty good seeing you these past few weeks. It truly brightened my life to have you around. Are you sure you won't reconsider and stay at the farm with us?"

Bill reached out and shook Thomas' hand. "I sure do appreciate the offer, Thomas, but you know I need to keep moving right now. One of these days you are going to look up and see me coming, and I'll be back for good then." He smiled and took a deep breath. "Once I get situated I'll send you a letter to let you know where I am. I do hope you'll write me and let me know how everyone is doing at Whitehall."

"I will, Bill," Thomas said with an embarrassed smile. "I promise I'll do better about my writing from here on out."

Neither one of the men knew who made the first move, but suddenly they both stepped forward and, while shaking hands, affectionately held each other on the upper arm with their other hand. It was the first time they had ever shown this kind of affection for each other, and they both knew immediately that their long relationship had created a very deep bond that had ultimately far surpassed the master and slave relationship. When they parted, both men felt lumps of emotion in their throats as they turned and went their own way.

—

With his pocket full of letters of recommendation and his experiences as a bellboy and cook, Bill quickly found that there were plenty of job opportunities in Savannah. After much thought he decided he would seek a job as a porter with the Charleston & Savannah Railroad. The railroad was a short line, only a little over one hundred miles, but it was a breathtakingly beautiful trip through Carolina farmlands, moss–draped cypress swamps, and lowland coastal marshes. After stopping at roughly a half dozen small towns or crossroads to pick up and drop off passengers, it would pull into Charleston about four hours later. Then it would turn around and return to Savannah, making the same run every day.

Bill had enjoyed his previous experiences with the railroad, so he felt that this would be a good way to make some money and enjoy himself while he was doing it. What he didn't expect, however, was the fact that the railroad was in such poor financial shape that he and the other workers would frequently not be paid for weeks.

By the summer of 1874, Bill was growing tired of the uncertainty about getting paid when he woke up one night with nausea, terrible chills, and a high fever. He managed to wake a friend who lived in the room next to him in their small Savannah boarding house and tell him of his plight. Upon seeing that Bill was extremely ill, he took him to Candler Hospital, where Bill was quickly diagnosed with malaria, a common and often deadly illness in the mosquito infested low country areas around Savannah and Charleston.

Over the next three weeks, Bill drifted in and out of consciousness and suffered excruciating headaches, vomiting, muscle aches, and constant fevers. The doctors, who were quite experienced with treating malaria, began quinine treatments on him, but for some reason he did not respond as quickly to the medicine as many others had. Bill's weight had dropped precariously from 150 pounds in early August to 105 pounds by mid September. The doctors felt certain he was going to die.

Hallucinations and vivid nightmares that he was once again in the Civil War plagued his unconsciousness. Day after day he thrashed and screamed in terror as he relived the horrors of the battlefields from his sweat–soaked bed. During many dreams, he would call out the names of some poor soul who had died during the war. In one dream, he found himself once again at the Battle of Seven Pines, holding onto Thomas as he dragged his wounded friend from the fiery battleground.

Bill gradually awoke. Through the swirling fog in his head, he could barely see Thomas' face and hear his distant voice calling to him through the dark veil of sweat and pain.

Bill cried out, "Masr, Masr, we've got to get out of this place before you get shot again. I'll help you."

"Bill, it's Thomas. We are not on the battlefield. I've come to take you back to Whitehall," Thomas said as he sat on the edge of the bed. He lightly shook Bill's frail arm.

As Bill's sunken, bloodshot eyes focused on the face, he gradually realized it was his old friend, and rather than him rescuing Thomas, the tables had turned. Thomas was here to take him home to Whitehall. He smiled for the first time in weeks and prayed that this was not just another dream.

"Thomas, you are here. Is it really you?" Bill whispered weakly as his hands grasped Thomas' hands.

"I'm right here, old friend," Thomas said as he held Bill's weak hand. He tried to smile. He had not expected to see Bill in such a bad condition, and it concerned him greatly.

—

Bill remembered little of the 115 mile wagon ride back to Dublin. Thomas had asked Bill's older sister, Constance, to come along and care for Bill during the journey. As the covered wagon bounced down the dusty Georgia roads, she sat in the back and kept cool damp rags on Bill's face. Whenever possible, she tried to feed him small amounts of food and water so that he could regain some of his strength. Bill was so malnourished and weak at that point that he could hardly lift his arms. His voice was so faint and frail that his sister had to put her ear to his mouth to hear his words.

Toward the end of their journey, Bill looked groggily into Thomas' face one evening as the campfire crackled beside them. "You know something, Masr, life's a powerful mystery. Only seems like yesterday when I was hauling you home in a wagon like this from Virginy. Now you are doing the same for me."

"That's what friends are for, Bill," Thomas said as he looked his friend in the eye. "I'll never be able to repay you for the kindness you have shown me over the years, and it makes me feel good to be able to help you."

Four days later, they made the turn from the main road onto the lane at Whitehall.

Everyone on the farm was horrified to see Bill in that condition. Many felt certain that he was going to die.

On one especially bad night, Miss Margaret sent for the circuit preacher to come and issue the final rites to Bill because they all felt he would only live for a few more hours. During those nights, all of the former slaves would sit around the fire outside of the small house where Bill lay, singing hymns and reciting prayers. Each of the women on the farm took turns sitting by Bill's side. William and Lia were constantly at his side.

With the love of his mother and father, the grace of God, and the constant attention of his friends and family, Bill slowly began to recuperate. By Thanksgiving, he was taking short walks with Thomas and had regained almost twenty pounds. He still looked extremely thin and feeble, but he was improving every day. His mother loved the challenge of "putting some meat on his scrawny bones" and piled his plate with food during every meal. Shortly before Christmas, he began doing light chores on the farm. By the end of January, his strength and stamina had fully returned, and he was ready to get on with his life.

During his recuperation, he and Thomas laughed at old jokes, reminisced about their days in the war, and had many long talks about other memorable experiences they had both shared. They also talked again about the irony of how Bill rescued Thomas from the battlefield in Virginia and now Thomas had done the same by bringing Bill home from certain death in Savannah. They finally agreed that God had put them both on this earth to help each other out of tough situations, somewhat like guardian angels. This was a comforting thought to the two men, and they smiled at the reassurance it brought.

—

Shortly after Bill's thirtieth birthday in July of 1875, he made the decision that it was time to move on once again. His plan this time was to return to New York to see what life in the North could offer. The thought of the bustling cities and the busy seaports pulled hard at him. Little did Bill know when he waved goodbye that before he returned home again, both of his parents would pass away.

THE SOFT SWEET MEMORIES
OF HIS LOVING HOME

By late 1875, Bill had made his way to Albany, New York, and had secured a job as a bellman at the most prominent hotel in town. His old friends at The Brown House Hotel had sent a letter to the owner of the hotel on Bill's behalf. It took no more than that to land the job. Once again, in short order, Bill became a favorite of the upper class elite and powerful politicians. After several years in town, he was even drafted by several political acquaintances to run for a city council position representing a minority district of the city. Bill's ability to make friends, his quick wit, and his innate intelligence endeared him to the powerful politicians in the city.

Through this process, Bill learned that he had a knack for public speaking. He enjoyed his frequent opportunities to help other people. With the strong support of his influential friends, he won the election in a landslide. After several years of public service, he grew weary of the political rat race and behind the scenes "dealings." He chose not to seek reelection. It was all too confining and no longer gratified him, so he tipped his hat in thanks to his associates, pulled up stakes once again, and moved on.

The 1880 Federal Census in Albany, New York, shows

that Bill was once again married. The woman was shown in the census as Mary J. Yopp, and she gave Albany, New York, as her birthplace. Just like Bill's first wife shown in the 1870 census, there is no further record of Mary and Bill being together in later census reports.

—

Several years went by as he tinkered with various jobs on the west coast. One record stated that he was a butler and chef for an extremely wealthy family in southern California for a portion of this time. He even traveled to Mexico several times to see what lay south of the border. In early 1888, he experienced a severe relapse of malaria, and his doctor suggested that he return to Albany and its cool, clear air to recuperate.

After arriving in Albany, he visited the manager of the hotel where he had previously worked. The man gladly gave Bill a room in which to spend several weeks recuperating. The combination of rest and cooler temperatures gave Bill more energy, and he used his new strength to reacquaint himself with old friends in the city.

Shortly after arriving in Albany, Bill was greeted by the news that another acquaintance of his, Mr. Reginald Browning, the President of the Delaware and Hudson Railroad, had requested that he come work for him as his personal porter and chef on his private train car. Bill was very fond of Mr. Browning, having gotten to know him when he frequented the hotel years earlier. Bill knew immediately that the job would offer him many great opportunities.

A strong bond had formed between Bill and Mr. Browning because they had a common love for hunting and fishing. No one around could cook wild game better than Bill. Each time Browning had scheduled a stay at the Albany hotel, Bill had made sure that the kitchen had all of his favorite wild game dishes, including pheasant, venison, and trout. That action had won the respect and admiration of Browning, which was leading to a new adventure. With the promise that he would be included on all of Mr. Browning's hunting and fishing trips, Bill excitedly accepted the job.

Bill's services for Mr. Browning must have given the railroad president much pleasure because one year later, during the summer of 1889, Browning presented Bill with an all expense paid trip to Europe. Browning had sensed Bill's love for travel and wanted to make that dream come true for his friend. Bill was overwhelmed at the gesture and quickly saw it as another great escapade to add to his growing list.

Bill traveled to Europe on "The City of Paris" steamship, which was considered one of the best luxury liners in the world. The trip included first class passage to London and to additional destinations such as Paris, Brussels, and Berlin. In each city Bill was greeted by friends and business associates of Browning, and the red carpet was rolled out for him. Bill became somewhat of a novelty within the elite circles of the European cities because of his status as a former slave who had overcome the bonds of captivity. They treated him like a great hero who had survived a life of evil domination and brutality. He was interviewed by several leading newspapers in Paris and London, with glowing articles being written about the little black man who had escaped the tyranny of slavery.

All of this was quite confusing and overwhelming to Bill. He could not understand why people made over him the way they did, but he went along with the festivities and enjoyed any opportunities afforded him. His trip lasted for over two months. During that time he wore fine clothes, toured famous landmarks, met dukes and duchesses and business leaders, dined in the best restaurants with the wealthy, and saw scenery unlike anything his mind could ever imagine. It seemed to him that the fairy tale trip could go on forever, but eventually he tired of the routine and longed for America and his real friends.

He returned to America on November 7, 1889, on a ship called *The City of New York*, which departed from Liverpool, England, and Queenstown, Ireland, for the voyage to America. Upon his return to Albany, Mr. Browning and many of his other friends threw a grand party for him, at which time he was asked to stand up and recount his travels through Europe. That type of event was a favorite pastime of the wealthy during the late nineteenth century. Whenever anyone took an exotic trip, everyone gathered to hear the tale of their travels in an effort to live the experience themselves. The fact that Bill was black and a former slave only heightened the excitement. It was a wonderful evening that Bill talked about until the day he died.

—

The next ten years were some of the happiest and most gratifying years of Bill's life. He regularly wrote letters to Thomas describing the wonderful duck and goose hunts or the amazing fishing trips. He and Mr. Browning frequently traveled into Canada for sport fishing or to Montana or Wyoming for big game hunting. During every adventure, Bill would prepare mouth–watering meals for Mr. Browning and his associates who had joined him for the trip. Whenever Bill was not busy cooking, Mr. Browning would take him into the woods or onto the water to enjoy the sport with him. Browning also enjoyed having Bill sit in his private car at night, recounting the tales of his war experiences and travels to Europe to his friends and associates. By then, Bill had become quite proficient at reciting the story of his life. He knew when to add in some humor or excitement to raise the lids of any weary eyes.

Then in 1897, without warning, Mr. Browning died of a heart attack. The private car was parked forever in a train yard. The death of Mr. Browning hit Bill hard because it not only meant the loss of a good friend but the end of his wonderful job.

At fifty two years old, Bill was once again on his own.

—

Not wanting to let any grass grow under his feet, Bill set out for southern California in 1898, just before his fifty-third birthday, to see what else that area of the country might hold for him. After only a few weeks, he made the momentous decision to join the U.S. Navy as a shipboard cook. This would be very different from his days cooking pheasant, salmon, and trout on Mr. Browning's private train car, but it afforded him the opportunity to see more of the world, something he had dreamed of since his trip to Europe.

From San Diego, he set sail on a five year round the world odyssey that took him from the Philippines to the South China Sea, from Australia to South Africa, and all major ports in between. Each time he was given a new ship assignment, he was quickly put in charge of the captain's mess and cooked his wonderful meals for the officers. In no time at all, Bill's reputation as the best captain's cook in the Navy spread far and wide. It was because of his close relationships with the top brass that he was given extra leave in most major cities where they docked. According to scanty records, Bill served most of his tour on a ship named the *USS Brutus,* a collier ship that transported coal and other supplies to US Naval bases around the world. This ship had an astonishing travel record and sailed to the four corners of the world from 1898 until it was decommissioned in 1921.

In each port, he would mail long letters to Thomas telling him of the wondrous sights he had seen, the food he had eaten, and the countries he had visited. Bill grew increasingly concerned when, in 1902, he realized that the last letter he had received from Thomas had been delivered in 1899. He had no idea what was happening in Georgia and wrote to Thomas with increasing urgency, all to no avail.

In Thomas' final letter, he sadly told of the death of Bill's mother and father within weeks of each other. Thomas recounted how Lia had passed away and William grieved himself to death. They were buried in the Whitehall slave cemetery. Thomas also vividly explained how the last words out of his mother's mouth proclaimed her love for Bill and the joy he had brought their family by becoming a man of the world.

—

As the clouds of World War One loomed over Europe in 1914, Bill realized that at sixty-nine years old, he had at last become an old man. He had seen more of the world than he ever imagined was possible during his sixteen years in the navy. He had met and befriended countless people from all walks of life. His had truly been a fulfilling and gratifying life, one of which he could forever be proud.

In his waning years, the soft, sweet memories of his warm home and loving family beckoned him to return to Whitehall. There he could relax and spend his final days sitting around the nightly campfire with his sisters and brothers and his old friend, Thomas.

NEXT STOP: DUBLIN, GEORGIA

1914

When Bill made the final decision to go home, he quickly learned that returning to his roots after a forty-year absence would generate an assortment of complex emotions ranging from excitement and joy to apprehension and fear. He experienced those feelings as soon as he stepped onto the homeward bound train in San Diego. A thousand questions raced through his head about what he would find at home. Finally, he took a deep breath and calmed himself by realizing that he was wasting his time and emotions by trying to second-guess the answers.

The long miles between San Diego and Dublin rolled quickly by. Before he knew it, the conductor called out, "next stop, Dublin, Georgia." Bill's adrenaline was pumping so strongly that he thought he would jump up and shout for joy. He sat on the edge of his seat and craned his neck in every direction, attempting to see what all had changed in Laurens County since the last time he rode out of there on a train bound for Albany, New York. At first glance, it all looked strangely different.

Soon after his arrival, he hired a man to drive him out to Whitehall in a buckboard wagon. Bill did not stop talking or asking questions of the wagon driver during the hour long trip out to the farm. He also frequently asked the man to drive faster. He was shocked at how much the town had grown and changed. He soon discovered that during his lengthy absence, the town and county had transformed into a strange and unfamiliar place. Many of the older brick buildings, such as the courthouse and the mercantile store, were still there, but there were also dozens of new streets and buildings that he had never seen.

As the wagon drew near to the first fields of Whitehall, Bill could tell that something was not right. The landscape looked dramatically different from the pictures he had stored in his memories. He thought that perhaps he was mistaken about his location. Relatively new small farmhouses dotted various corners of the property where the huge cotton fields had once been. Strangers, both black and white, stared quizzically at Bill and the passing wagon from every front porch.

Up ahead he recognized the sprawling oak trees that lined the main road to Whitehall. The familiar sight made him feel better. The old trees greeted him with their familiar beauty and comforting shade. When he caught a glimpse of the roof of the Yopps' big house, his pulse quickened. He strained his eyes to get a better look. He expected to see a swarm of children come racing down the road at any moment, calling his name.

The wagon turned down the cool, shady lane. There to his left, like a long lost friend, stood the large, old magnolia tree. Bill smiled at his aged friend as he rode by. As the wagon drew closer to the big house, he was stunned to see that the yard was completely overgrown, and the house appeared abandoned. Grass and brush grew tall in the yard. The weathered skeletons of two old farm wagons sat rotting under an oak tree near the front door. The moss–covered remnants of two ropes hung from an oak limb, and Bill remembered that was where the children used to swing for hours.

Windows were missing from the grand old house, and the front door stood ajar, as if the last person who walked out forgot to close it. Wisteria vines had slowly snaked their way up the outside of the brick chimneys and now covered almost half of the roof, crawling into every crack and crevice. Whitehall Plantation was void of life. The home's past glory was just a whisper on the wind that rustled through the oaks and tall grass.

"Don't look like nobody has lived here for quite a while," the wagon driver said in a matter–of–fact manner. He took a draw from his corncob pipe and blew the smoke into the sky. "You sure this is the right place?"

"Yes, it's the right place. This is where I grew up," Bill said in a low, concerned voice. "I'd appreciate it if you would wait for a while. I need to look around. It looks like I may need a ride back into town with you."

"Yes, sir, I'll be happy to wait," the driver replied.

"Thank you. I'll try not to be too long," Bill said.

Bill slowly climbed from the wagon and walked up the rotting front steps. A rush of fond memories whirled through his mind as he approached the large door. A knot of nagging fear and mystery swirled through his head regarding the whereabouts of Thomas and of his own family members. He hoped to see their smiling faces at any minute. The questions stuck hard in his chest.

Someone had removed or stolen the two large brass lanterns from either side of the front door. They had always been such a welcome beacon to Bill, like a lighthouse in a storm. He reached up and ran his fingers across the holes where the lanterns had been mounted to the walls. He then stepped through the front door and was bewildered to see that the house was completely vacant except for a few old wooden boxes and several bales of hay that some farmer had placed in the drawing room. Cobwebs draped the corners like lacy streamers from some recent celebration. He stopped and listened carefully, hoping he would hear the squeals and laughter of children or the familiar old songs of the slaves. However, all he heard was the nearby cooing of several pigeons that had been roosting in an open closet in the parlor.

As Bill stepped further into the foyer, the pigeons flew frantically across the parlor and through a broken window. They took Bill's breath away with fright. Several feathers ripped loose during their frantic escape floated slowly to the floor in the sun–streaked dusty air.

The strong odor of dust and mildew filled his nostrils and convinced him that Thomas and the family had been gone for quite some time. He looked down at the dirt–covered hardwood floor and remembered the countless times he had swept this exact spot. It troubled him to see it as it was today.

He slowly walked through the dining room and out the open back door. He headed in the direction of the cookhouse and the small home where he and his family had lived. A jolt of surprise shot through his body as he looked up and saw that the cookhouse where he had spent so many happy hours with his mother had burned to the ground. Nothing but old blackened timbers, the falling brick chimney, and tall weeds growing through the floorboards could be seen.

Fifty yards to the rear of the cookhouse, he saw the crumbling remains of the shanty that had been his home. He quickly walked through the tall broom straw grass and pushed the honeysuckle vines out of the way to get a closer look. Blackberry briars grabbed at his pants legs with every step, and he winced at the pain as several of them ripped at his skin. It appeared that the roof of the old shanty had rotted and caved in. All he could see through the weed–choked open door was the decaying frame of his mother's bed and the remnants of some other furniture. A brown rabbit skittered across the weed–covered floor and out through a hole in the far wall. Forlornly he joked to himself that at least something still called this place home.

His eyes wandered around the expansive property and settled on the small tree–covered knoll located several hundred yards to the rear of the house, where the old slave cemetery was located. After walking for several minutes through the familiar weed–covered field, he stood next to the concrete and brick slab that covered his mother's grave. Someone had scrawled her name and date of death into the wet mortar with a stick. Bill kneeled beside the slab. He traced the letters that spelled *Helia Yopp* with his forefinger as he tried to envision her sweet face and infectious smile. He noticed the remnants of an old clay flowerpot at the head of his mother's grave and felt certain his father had grievingly placed it there before his death. He tenderly ran his fingers across the small pot in hopes of feeling something that would connect his broken heart to theirs, but it did little to help. He felt a tightening rush of sadness and loneliness. He missed them both, missed it all quite desperately. He trembled as he breathed deeply.

His father's grave lay beside hers. Choking weeds three feet tall grew around it. Bill brushed off several limbs and a thick layer of rotting leaves and vines to read his name. Taking a deep and sorrowful breath, he stood beside the two graves and began talking to his parents.

"Mama and Daddy, it's Bill. I have finally come home after all of these years, and I wanted to tell you that I miss both of you something terrible." He paused. "Mama," he said, turning to look at her grave, "I'm very sorry that I stayed away so long without coming home to check on you. Thomas was writing every now and then and letting me know how you were doing. He said that he was taking good care of you, and you know how I trust old Thomas. I hope you enjoyed the money I sent you and some of the presents."

Bill paused, took a deep breath again, and continued.

"Y'all would both be real proud of me for all that I have done since I left Whitehall. I have traveled all over this big world and seen things that were amazing. I have been a good God–fearin' man and tried to go to church every week. I helped people out whenever I could. I always tried to live just the way you both told me."

He stopped and took a long, expansive look around the old home.

"I'm not real sure what I'm going to do with myself right now. I may go back to Macon and try to get a job there. That was a nice town. I'm going to try to find Thomas, but I'm not real sure where to start looking. Well, I better go. I'll come back to see you soon. I love you both."

With that said, Bill slowly and awkwardly kneeled down in front of the graves. He leaned over, planted a kiss on his fingers, and then, one by one, placed them on the cold mortar of the tombstones. As he stood up, a tear dripped from his eyes and splashed onto his mother's grave.

—

Bill walked around the remnants of Whitehall for another thirty minutes. He visited the ruins of the old slave quarters and other farm outbuildings. Everything he saw brought back a flood of memories and made him long for the days of his carefree childhood. Each time he saw something familiar, a lump of breathlessness rose into his chest. The only way to relieve it was to breathe deeply and move on. He had never realized that heartache could be so painful.

He unhurriedly gazed across the weed–choked fields toward the creek bottom where he and Thomas had spent so many happy hours hunting and fishing. He knew that he would never enjoy those things again. The unending sights of his lost memories saddened him greatly. It all seemed so very, very old and long ago.

—

During the trip back to Dublin, Bill had the driver stop at several houses so that he could ask for information about Thomas and the other people who had lived at Whitehall. Many folks knew who Thomas was and said that the Yopp family had fallen on hard times No one knew where the family had gone. One old man told Bill that about half of Whitehall had gradually been sold off to tenant farmers. Additionally, Thomas had borrowed against the remainder of the farm and had eventually lost it to the bank. Bill couldn't believe that Thomas no longer owned Whitehall.

As a last resort, Bill asked the wagon driver to drop him off at the post office in Dublin, where he went inside and asked the postmaster if Thomas had left any forwarding information. Much to his dismay, the postmaster said he did not know where Thomas was. In fact, he had a small stack of letters addressed to Thomas that he was holding in the event he returned. Bill asked to see the letters. He was surprised and disheartened to see that all of the letters he had sent to Thomas for the last two years were in this stack. Before leaving the post office, Bill told the postmaster that as soon as he settled down, he would like to send a letter to him explaining how to get in touch with him in case Thomas returned. The old postmaster was most agreeable and wished him well with his search.

Bill walked out to the busy main street in Dublin and stared at the bustling activity. He felt completely alone and confused. He had come home to spend his final years in the happy, comfortable surroundings of Whitehall, but there was no more Whitehall. He had come home to see his brothers and sisters and their children, to have nieces and nephews call him Uncle Bill. He had imagined the satisfaction he would get from sitting under a big tree and telling stories to the children about sailing the oceans and visiting Japan, China, and India. That would not happen. From all indications, his family had split up into several groups, with some living in South Carolina and others in small, rural communities around Georgia. Most importantly, he had come home to be with Thomas to share the joys and memories of their lives together. However, Thomas had disappeared, and he had no clues where to start looking for him.

His grand plan for the remainder of his life was in shambles.

RIDING ON THE "ONE SPOT"

AUGUST 1914

ill rented a room in Dublin. He spent several distressing and frustrating days going door to door, trying to determine the whereabouts of Thomas and his family. He also spent countless hours sitting in a rocking chair and looking out his boarding house window while his mind conjured up various plans for what his next move would be. The only shred of information he found regarding Thomas was from another old man who had been in The Blackshear Guards with them during the Civil War. The man thought he remembered hearing someone say that Thomas was living in Atlanta, but he wasn't sure.

Four days of fruitless searching in Dublin combined with the disheartening realization that he was a genuine stranger in his own hometown resulted in Bill packing up his bag and purchasing a train ticket to Savannah. He had learned that The Central of Georgia Railroad ran daily between Savannah and Atlanta. A job with the railroad could give him the opportunity he needed to begin his search for Thomas in Atlanta.

—

Upon arrival in Savannah, Bill went directly to the main office of the Central of Georgia and applied for a job as a porter. As he presented his credentials to the young personnel screener, Bill gave him a letter from the Vice President of the Delaware and Hudson Railroad extolling his capabilities as a chef and porter on the private car of the president of the railroad. As soon as the young man read the letter, he began smiling. He looked up at Bill and said, "Sometimes the good Lord does us all favors."

Perplexed, Bill said, "I'm sorry. I don't quite understand your meaning."

"Mr. Yopp, this is quite a coincidence of good timing and good luck." He leaned back in his chair. "The superintendent of the railroad, Mr. Marion Ramsey, sent a request to me just this week to hire a new porter and chef for his private car. In all my years of interviewing applicants for the railroad, I have never seen anyone who fits the job description better than you. We should set up a meeting between you and Mr. Ramsey as soon as possible."

—

One week later Bill boarded the "One Spot," which was the name for the most famous private car on the Central of Georgia railroad. The posh car traveled all over the 1,500 miles of Central of Georgia tracks throughout Georgia, Alabama, and Tennessee. It regularly carried executives of the railroad to and from major cities. After the first few days of traveling with Bill, Mr. Ramsey knew that Bill was someone special. He thanked his lucky stars for delivering Bill to his railroad. From Bill's perspective, he couldn't have asked for a better job because it allowed him to continue with the life of travel that he loved. Additionally, he would get a free day or two in Atlanta at least once every two weeks.

Months went by and Bill made repeated trips to Atlanta searching for his old friend. Each time the train stopped, he would hire a wagon to take him to a place that had been recently suggested by some caring soul. He had been to the police department and asked for help, but he got very few ideas. He checked out dozens of boarding houses. He even ran an advertisement in the Atlanta newspaper, but he got no replies. He had also visited most of the hospitals, and no one had any records of a Thomas Yopp.

Every lead turned frustratingly cold until one chilly morning in December. Bill was asking several railroad executives questions about Atlanta. As he served their breakfast on the One Spot, he explained that he was trying to find an old friend he had known during the war. He wondered if they had any ideas where an old man might go who had no family in Atlanta. Several thoughts were thrown out, but the one that tweaked Bill's interest was the mention of a place called "The Georgia Confederate Soldiers' Home." It was a state run home where a large group of destitute old Confederate soldiers lived. In all of his searches, that place had never been mentioned. He could not imagine Thomas being penniless and felt certain that his former master would not be living on charity. Despite his pessimism about this new lead, he set off for the home as soon as the train stopped in the rail yard.

—

As Bill fumbled in his pocket for the cab fare, he couldn't take his eyes off the massive building sitting on a slight hill a hundred yards off the street. Rather than having the driver take the circular driveway leading to the front door, he asked to stop on the street so he could take in the grandeur of the home. Four massive, white, Ionic columns dominated the front of the two–story, red brick building. The doors were trimmed with fresh paint. Most of the tall windows were open to let in the cool morning air. The home reminded him of the grand plantation houses that he knew too well from his childhood.

A dozen bearded, old men had already staked out their favorite rocking chairs on the smaller covered porches. From where he stood he counted six towering brick chimneys that were spread out across various areas of the gray slate roof. A large white lettered sign over the doorway read "Confederate Soldier's Home."

Before mounting the wide wooden steps on the front porch he took a deep breath and said a short prayer that his friend Thomas was here. The large screen door squealed as he opened it and stepped into a huge foyer. The ceilings were over twenty feet tall and graceful curved stairways swept up on either side to the second floor. A sparrow that had flown inside earlier was fluttering around the large, brass light fixture in the ceiling making him wonder how long it would be trapped there. He immediately noticed that the room had a distinct odor. It was like the unforgettable scent of a place where old folks lived. Part mildew, part dust, a faint aroma of liniment, and the smell of really old things.

Looking past the large foyer, he could see a long, dimly lit hallway where two elderly men were hobbling along at a slow pace. Both of them had on big, floppy hats, and Bill suspected they wore these more from the habit than the need to protect their eyes from the sun. Bill stood entranced watching the two men help each other down the long hallway. They took childlike steps and were in no hurry. Bill knew that he had a common bond with these men. They too had fought in the Civil War.

From some unseen corner of the building, he could barely hear the lilting, throaty sounds of an angelic female voice coming from a scratchy phonograph record. The melancholy song professed a woman's love for a soldier who never returned from war in some distant land. Bill thought how appropriate this was in the current setting.

Rising above the music, from another area of the building, he heard the unsettling wail of an old man who kept calling a woman's name.

"Ava! Ava! I'm home. Where are you?"

Another elderly voice replied harshly, "Shet up, you crazy old bastard. Ye ain't home, and Ava ain't nowhere around here!"

Bill never liked it when the truth was so blunt. He wished he could somehow ease the old man's sorrow, but he knew he could not. The anguished pain of misplaced memories was buried deeply in his heart and mind——where no one could reach them.

An open station with a chest high counter was on the right side of the foyer. A printed sign read, "Guests, Please Check in Here," stood on the desk next to a small, brass hand bell. Bill rang the bell gently, not wanting to make any more noise than necessary.

Within seconds an overweight gray-headed nurse in a tight uniform walked through a rear door into the small outer office area.

"How can I help you, Sir?" she said. She smiled pleasantly.

"Thank you, ma'am," Bill said. He smiled. As usual, he was dressed smartly in his dark suit and held his hat in his hands. "My name is Bill Yopp, and I am here to see if an old friend named Thomas McCall Yopp is by chance living here."

The nurse smiled and responded quickly.

"Yes, Mr. Yopp. We do have a Thomas Yopp living here, but, uh, he is a white gentleman," she replied, somewhat confused. "Our Mr. Yopp has been with us for a little over six years, I believe."

"Yes ma'am," he replied. His pulse quickened with anticipation. "The man I'm lookin' for is white, not colored. He's around 85 years old by now."

"That sounds like him," the nurse said.

His heart skipped a beat and his face beamed with happiness. The nurse could tell that she had just made Bill a very happy man.

"Why don't you come with me, Mr. Yopp, and we'll go find him." She waved her arm in the direction of a long hallway. "His room is right down here. We'll see if he is in there. If not, he may be in the reading room or the game room."

The nurse asked several questions about Bill's background and his relationship to Thomas as they walked down the long hallway. When Bill explained that he had been a slave at Whitehall and that Thomas had been his master, she shook her head in disbelief at what was unfolding in front of her. Several times Bill had to slow down because, in his haste to see Thomas, he was walking faster than the nurse. Finally, they came to a room that the nurse said belonged to Thomas. She knocked on the door and listened, but there was no response. She slowly opened the door and looked in.

"Oh, Mr. Yopp," Bill could hear the nurse say in a surprised tone as she looked through the doorway. "I wasn't sure if you were in here. You have a guest."

The nurse looked at Bill with a big smile as she motioned for him to come into the room. The bedroom was fairly large and contained two single beds and two small desks with chairs. It was all very neat and sparse. A slumped over elderly man wearing a dark suit and a rumpled hat was sitting in one of the chairs. He was looking out the large, sunny window.

Bill slowly walked into the room and stopped several feet away from the man who was slowly turning to see who could be coming to visit him. As soon as Thomas saw

Bill standing in the middle of the room, he recognized his face.

"Masr, it's Bill. I can't believe I have finally found you. This is the greatest day of my life," he exclaimed. Tears welled up in his eyes as he walked closer to Thomas. The old man began rising out of his chair with the help of a walking cane to face his friend.

"Bill. Bill Yopp, is it really you?" Thomas asked, a wide smile on his wrinkled face. "I have thought about you almost every day since you left and wondered if we would ever see each other again. I sure have missed you, my old friend."

With that said, Bill and Thomas walked toward each other and embraced as only two lifelong friends can. They hugged and patted each other on the back. They stepped back to look more closely at each other and hugged again.

"Well, I'll leave you two alone," the happy nurse said. "If you need anything, just let me know."

Bill could see the pool of tears in her eyes.

Bill walked over and picked up an old ladder–backed chair. He sat it down in front of the one Thomas had been sitting in and told his old master to have a seat. They sat almost knee–to–knee and hardly knew what to say to each other. Tears of joy ran down both of their cheeks as they sat and stared into each other's eyes for the first time in over forty years. Thomas reached for Bill's hand and held it tightly.

The two friends sat and jabbered like school children

for hours about what all had happened with their lives over the past four decades. They laughed aloud, telling old stories about life at Whitehall or humorous things that had happened during the war. The conversation swung from excited descriptions of Bill's travels around the world to sad explanations from Thomas about losing Whitehall Plantation during the 1870s. In a sullen and despondent voice, Thomas explained how he had moved from job to job for several years and eventually ended up in Runnels County, Texas, working on a large ranch for a man named Robert Wylie during the 1880s. He had invested his few remaining dollars in a cattle operation that failed. He left Texas penniless and returned to Georgia. Thomas lived for short periods in Polk and Carroll counties doing odd jobs and living off the generosity of friends. By 1908, Thomas, now eighty–two years old, was sickly and completely destitute. His only chance for living out his remaining years in a dignified manner was to turn to the Confederate Soldier's Home in Atlanta, which he entered in the spring of 1908.

As soon as Bill gathered enough information to understand that Thomas was a broken and penniless man, he tried to change the subject to more pleasant items of discussion. He did not want Thomas to have to dwell on the gut–wrenching details that had obviously saddened and disheartened him. Bill could plainly see that each time Thomas began talking about the downfall of Whitehall, his eyes would become glassy, and he would stare off into the distance as if he were in some hypnotic trance.

When the lunch bell rang around noon, Thomas invited Bill to join him in the dining room. They continued their childish banter as they walked down the hallway to the dining room. They soon took seats at a large dinner table filled with other men.

Immediately following the blessing, which was given by an elderly minister, Thomas stood up and introduced Bill to the ninety–seven men who lived there. Throughout the meal a steady stream of men hobbled over to Bill and shook his hand, welcoming him to the home. There were several men who knew Bill from the old Blackshear Guards, and they all had a happy reunion talking about their days during the war.

"We have heard old Yopp and these other fellers talk about you many times," one man said. "We thought they was just making it all up, his talk about you being the best cook in the state of Georgia and about you running out onto the battlefields to rescue folks. We also heard that they called you 'Ten Cent Bill'." Everyone that heard this comment laughed. The conversation continued in a happy tone until they finished eating.

"Yes, suh," Bill answered. "It's all true. And I can still shine your shoes for ten cents if you want me to."

One man spoke up, saying, "We'd let you shine our shoes if we had ten cents." The other men chuckled at the hard truth.

Everyone in the room laughed and smiled. It was good medicine for the old soldiers who now lived a life of solitary boredom.

As the joyous afternoon progressed, it became obvious to Bill that these men lived a very Spartan lifestyle. They had little, if any, money and could not afford to buy themselves even the smallest items, such as new socks or underwear, a pouch of tobacco, or writing paper for letters to their few remaining friends and family. Thomas explained to Bill that a stipulation of them entering the home was that the men had to forfeit their state military pensions. They were all legally bankrupt. It distressed Bill to see that his old master, who had lived most of his life in a grand house with money and servants, was in a situation where he did not even have a nickel to buy a newspaper.

It was obvious that this lifestyle was depressing and demeaning to the proud warriors, so Bill began formulating a plan to bring some light and pleasure back into their lives.

A GENERATION OF LOST SOULS

Bill returned to the Soldiers' Home ten times over the next six months. During each visit to Atlanta, he would stop at the market to purchase items such as fresh fruit, clothes, an occasional fresh pie or cake, and pipe tobacco for Thomas. If he knew of an item another soldier needed badly, he would frequently buy that, too. He regularly hired a young boy to help him carry everything back to the home. Soon the men jokingly began calling him Santa Claus, and the young boy was his elf.

Bill did not make much money as a porter, but he did not spend much money on his lifestyle, either. It was obvious that he received his greatest enjoyment from doing good deeds for his old friends. Every time he walked into Thomas' room with an armload of gifts, he made certain to present them as special presents tied to a holiday or birthday so that Thomas would not feel that Bill was doing this to help out a poor old man. Thomas would not have accepted a single gift from Bill if he had felt they were handouts to the needy. When he brought food, Bill always said, "Thomas, I brought *us* some fresh apples and oranges so that *we* would have something to eat when I come visit you." Bill was not sure if Thomas noticed that he never ate any of the fruit while he was there.

—

In the early fall of 1916, Mr. Ramsey notified Bill that the Central of Georgia would be increasing their passenger loads of soldiers who were coming and going to army training camps or heading off to the great war in Europe. As much as it pained him, he had to tell Bill that they could no longer afford to keep the private car on the rail line. Bill had a choice of either staying on as a porter on the Pullman Sleeper Cars or resigning. Realizing that he was too old to keep the long hours on the Pullman Cars, Bill decided to leave to find other employment. During his last day on the job, Mr. Ramsey gave Bill an envelope with a twenty–five dollar bonus for his good work and told him to stay in touch in case something changed. He also gave Bill a letter stating that if he ever needed to travel, he could ride on the Central of Georgia at no charge.

Shortly before leaving the railroad, Bill had a stopover one night in Macon, Georgia. He went to visit a prominent man, W. T. Anderson, the new publisher of *The Macon Daily Telegraph*. Bill knew that Mr. Anderson had a soft spot in his heart for the plight of blacks during this period of continued segregation. In fact, in 1917 W.T. Anderson became one of the first newspaper publishers in the U.S. to institute an exclusive page of the newspaper for news from the black community, with its own black editor. This section was so popular that it lasted until 1969 when it was discontinued as one of the last vestiges of segregation.

Anderson was a very independent thinker for his times and often stood his ground even when threatened with violence. He dared to criticize and denounce the Ku Klux Klan at the height of its power in the 1920s and 1930s. His editorials called for equal justice and educational opportunities for blacks, even after his life had been threatened and crosses had been burned on his lawn.

After Anderson's death in 1945, in his final gesture to assist the black community, his estate left much of his considerable wealth to help indigent blacks receive medical care.

Bill confidently walked into the newspaper that morning and asked to see Mr. Anderson. After explaining his background, the receptionist sent him up to Anderson's office. When Bill walked into the big office, he was astounded by the positive reaction he received from Anderson. It didn't take the young publisher very long to realize that Bill was a very special man with an amazing history. An hour later, Bill finished telling the man about his life on the plantation, the Civil War, and his odyssey around the world. He then stated his purpose for the visit was that he would soon be looking for a job and wondered if he knew of anything around Macon that an old man like him could do to earn a living. Anderson was in awe of Bill's accomplishments and his references from powerful people all over the U.S. and was more than willing to help him. He told Bill to stop back by his office the next time he was in town, and he would have some news for him.

—

Two weeks later, during Bill's next visit to Macon, Anderson told Bill that he had found him a job as the chef in the Officer's Club at the nearby army base, Camp Wheeler. Anderson set up a meeting at the club for Bill and told him to stay in touch. Bill was very appreciative and took a cab out to the sprawling camp, where over thirty thousand soldiers were in training for the Great War in Europe.

Bill was given his own room in the Officer's Club and was put in charge of six cooks in the big kitchen. Before long he had the men preparing such incredible dishes that the officers found themselves needing to make reservations on weekends in order to get a seat for dinner. Bill's cuisine was a hit, and his personal service was the best any of these men had ever seen. One night during Bill's first week on the job, as he went for an evening walk on the army base, he laughed to himself and thought how ironic it was that at seventy–one–years–old, he was in the Army again.

—

One of the many benefits of Bill's new job was that he received a day and a half off from work each week as well as certain holidays. He was even given several weeks of paid vacation as a gift from the Commanding General, who respected Bill's situation and age. During one of his days away from work, Bill went to see his friend, Mr. Anderson, at the newspaper to tell him how his new job was progressing and to invite him out to the camp for dinner one night. He also had a grand plan that he wanted to discuss with him.

"Well, Bill," Anderson said as he lit up a cigar and sat down in his big desk chair, "I keep hearing rave reviews about the food you are preparing out at the camp. I knew you would like it out there."

"Thank you, Mr. Anderson," Bill said politely. "I don't know if my cookin' is all that good. It's just that them poor boys was eating some mighty awful stuff before I got there."

Anderson laughed, and they chatted for a few minutes before Bill presented his idea to the publisher.

"Mr. Anderson," Bill said as he sat up straighter in his chair, "You remember that I was telling you about finding my old Masr in the Confederate Soldier's Home in Atlanta?"

"Yes, I remember that, Bill. That was an amazing piece of detective work you did."

"Well, suh, I have been going up there almost every month this past year, and I have been finding out some troubling things that need to be changed. There are over ninety fine old soldiers up there who fought for the South. They gave up just about everything they had in the process. Lots of these men lost an arm or a leg. Others are deaf or blind. The state of Georgia done taken away what little pension they got, so now they don't have a penny to even buy themselves a chew of tobacco. It's a real shame that these heroes are being treated like this. I would like to ask if you and your fine newspaper can help me to raise some money to give to these men at Christmastime."

Without having to think about it, Anderson jumped up from his desk, smiled, and replied, "Bill, I think that is a marvelous idea. In fact, if we handle this correctly, we can set it up so that everyone in the state can send in his or her nickels or dimes if they would like to help these old soldiers out." Anderson's brain had kicked into high gear, and his mind raced with new ideas for how to organize and promote the project.

"Here's what we'll do, Bill." Anderson paced energetically around his office. "I'll meet with our editorial staff and we'll come up with a plan. You can come back over here in a week, and we'll discuss it with you. I'm sure we'll want to interview you to find out more about your life, Thomas Yopp, and the men at the home."

Bill was smiling from ear to ear.

"This is like a gift from heaven," Bill said. He smiled and looked toward the ceiling. "This will be wonderful to help these old men out. I think you'll see pretty quickly that there will be lots of interest from the good folks in Georgia."

On Saturday morning, October 27, 1917, *The Macon Daily Telegraph* ran their first newspaper article about Bill's project to raise money for his old friends at the

Confederate Soldier's home. This article ran on the front page.

Ante–Bellum Negro

Finds Old Master in Soldier's Home
"Ten Cent" Bill has been Playing
Commissary for One Whom he Went to War
With.
Telegraph takes up the Case and Plans to
Raise $100 to help him Continue his Work.

They called him "Ten Cent Bill" in the days of the sixties all through Virginia and straight on through to Appomattox the then slender young Negro who left Laurens County, Georgia with his young master when the first call came for volunteers to wear the gray. When Young Master went, of course Bill went along and he soon became handy man and servant of the whole company. Every dime they got they gave to Bill and so he came to be known as Ten–Cent Bill or just "Ten" for short.

Not every man who surrendered with Lee at Appomattox came back to his home state to rebuild a fortune and die in plenty. The rigors of those years took more from so many men than a starved and ravaged country could ever put back in them during the lean years of an enforced peace. And so Young Marster didn't do so well in all the decades that followed that sorrowful march home. "Ten–Cent" Bill had to leave if he would eat, and so the wandering foot that followed the Georgia company in Lee's Army of Virginia wandered over many lands.

They All Knew Him

Britain, France, the Orient, the lands that lie below the Southern Cross…they all came to know Ten–Cent Bill. He came to cook with rare skill and was born with that deference to the white man that marks the servant who is never discharged from his service.

Ten–Cent Bill turned up some months ago in Georgia, and about that time Marion Ramsay, superintendent of the Macon division of the Central of Georgia was looking for a man to cook and make up beds in his private car. Ten–Cent Bill asked for the job, showed in his quiet way that he could cook, and got it. It would be a hard matter to get Ten Cent out of the old "One–Spot" for several years. As intimated before, he knows how to serve white folks.

Finds Old Master.

Bill a while back got into the habit of asking for an hour or so off every time the car went to Atlanta which was quite often and it became known that old Ten Cent wasn't saving much money. He needed his paycheck when it came. For one day the old Negro made a discovery in Atlanta. He found out there was an Old Soldiers' Home there and he wandered out that way. There might be some of the Laurens County men with whom he campaigned in Virginia.

There he found his Young Marster…but Ole marse now, 86 years old, sitting in the sunshine each day dreaming the hours away, half–lost in the days, the great old days of over half a century ago. You see, things didn't go well with Young Marster when he came back—which is why Ten–Cent Bill lost him for so long.

Ten–Cent took a good look around, examined the cuisine and found it didn't suit him in any particular way. It didn't seem to be the kind of food that his white folks, or any Georgian who fought with Lee, ought to have in the declining years of a very old age. So he went off down town and loaded up a basket with tea and sugar and fruit and all sorts of things that he knew young soldiers liked to have and old soldiers needed in the soldiers' home.

Commissary Committee of One

And that's what Ten–Cent Bill has been doing with a large portion of his wages for quite some time now. He is a commissary committee of one to Young Marster and some of his comrades and the forage comes from Bill's pocketbook. All his money above bare living expenses goes that way.

But to Bill's notion even an augmented commissary isn't enough for the men who fought straight through with Mr. Lee. He found out in this connection that the old gentlemen who mainly sit out in the sun out there would like to see picture shows once in awhile, would like to get down–town in Atlanta and get all sorts of little things in the way of extra tobacco and newspapers and so on, that they must supply from private funds they haven't got.

Bill thinks the white folks down around this part of the state should do something about it and he put it up to the Telegraph to lay the matter before them; and to back it up he dug down and put up a dollar to head the list, a list that the Telegraph is going to see through to $100. When the funds are raised the money will be dispatched to Atlanta by William H. Yopp, "Ten–Cent" Bill, who fought all through Virginia over 50 years ago, and has seen a lot of the world since–and found Young Marster one idle day up there in Atlanta.

The list is started herewith:
William H. Yopp $1.00
W.T. Anderson $1.00
George H. Long $1.00
Total= $3.00

(It ought to take about two issues of the paper only to get this hundred.)

Bill and the people at the newspaper office were caught off guard by the immediate outpouring of sympathy and money that flooded in from caring Georgians. Within one week of when the original article was published, the newspaper office had received over one hundred dollars. The money and letters continued to pour in. During Thanksgiving week, the newspaper reprinted the original article and attached to it a complete list of all of the donors with how much money they had given. Letters with pennies collected by children were received. Churches took up special offerings and donated their dollars with blessings to the soldiers. One poor soul actually placed a stamp on a silver dollar coin and mailed it to the newspaper. Some of the officers at the army base where Bill worked got into the act and began collecting money. They sent in fifteen dollars and signed it, "The officers and men at Camp Wheeler who pray that when they are old soldiers, there will be another Bill Yopp there to help them."

On December 20, 1917, Mr. Anderson ran an article stating that the fundraising drive was over and that they had collected almost two hundred dollars, double the amount they had hoped for. That meant that each of the ninety–seven men at the home would receive $2.06, enough to buy plenty of small items that they each needed. The gift would give them a very merry Christmas.

Mr. Anderson, Bill, and the superintendent of the soldiers' home decided that Christmas Eve would be the most fitting time for Bill to present the money to the men at the home. Bill met with Thomas and the other soldiers in the small chapel at the home immediately following their Christmas Eve dinner. A dozen invited dignitaries were in attendance, and several reporters from area newspapers were there, too.

After all of the men and employees of the home shuffled into the small chapel and took a seat, the superintendent, William McAllister, walked to the pulpit and spoke.

"I want to thank each of you for coming here tonight for a very special event in the history of the Soldier's Home. I think that most of you know Bill Yopp by now, and you are aware of all of the wonderful things he has done for you and the home. In fact, he put together your Christmas dinner tonight, and I think it was one of the best meals we have ever had here." A round of applause rose from the group of aged soldiers. Weak voices could be heard above the noise, proclaiming their agreement and thanks to Bill.

"As all of you know, Bill has recently enlisted the aid of the publisher of *The Macon Daily Telegraph* to raise money for Christmas presents for each of you from the citizens of Georgia. I would like for Bill to come up here now and tell you about the campaign."

With that, McAllister turned to Bill and motioned for him to come to the pulpit.

As Bill stood from his front row seat, a rumble of applause began in the rear of the room and moved slowly forward. Bill climbed the short steps to the pulpit as the applause grew louder. The men began standing. Cheers could be heard over the applause. "Thanks, Bill!" "God bless you, Ten Cent!" The applause continued for several more seconds until Bill raised his hands. In a shy and embarrassed tone, he told the men to have a seat. Within seconds the room was totally quiet. The short black man, in a dark suit and white shirt with tie, looked out at his old friends and spoke.

"I come to you tonight as an emissary from all those people across this great state who fondly remember you as a small army of old heroes whose memory they cherish and whose sacrifices and loyalty in a country's cause will live forever. You represent the bravest of the brave and the generation of lost souls who fought for a cause that will never be forgotten. I have been blessed during my long life to meet many folks who have made great sacrifices, but I have never met a group who has given more than you. With that said, I am truly happy tonight to give each of you over two dollars from the fine people of the state of Georgia. They send this money to you with love and respect for what you have endured. They hope that your Christmas will be a happy one. Thank you for the friend-ship and kindness you have each shown me. If you ever need anything, just call old Ten and I'll be there for you."

When he stepped away from the pulpit, the group once again stood and began clapping with appreciation and love for the old man. One by one the soldiers filed by the front of the dimly lit chapel to shake Bill's hand and receive the money he had brought them. After that evening, many who attended said that it was one of the most moving outpourings of love that they had ever seen.

—

Over the next several years, the fundraising drive started by Bill and promoted by the Macon newspaper grew larger and larger. People from all backgrounds became involved and pitched in pennies to help the old soldiers. In November of 1918, a particularly inspiring letter was written by a man from Macon named W. L. Williams. It was sent to the editor of *The Macon Daily Telegraph.*

To the Editor,

The scripture says something about us being taught wisdom by babes. I am also persuaded that often we are taught some things by those in the humble walks of life. I was born on a Georgia plantation. I grew up more or less among the Negroes of the place and always hold for the race the very kindest of feelings. Georgia has provided a home for our old Confederate Veterans and doubtless they are well fed and cared for. Some of them are surely without Kith or Kin and their lot is not altogether one of sunshine and roses. It has been left to an ex-slave of one of these old heroes to teach our descendants of Confederate Soldiers that it was possible to add a little more joy and happiness in these old fellows' lives. "Ten-Cent Bill" is a dandy and I hereby move, second, and carry unanimously that his name be changed to "Dollar Bill." Nothing smaller is large enough for a Negro of his caliber.

I am enclosing my check for his fund for one dollar and doing so I wish to appeal to all Sons of Confederate Veterans everywhere. I wish all grandsons, daughters and grand–daughters to do likewise and lets raise a sum that will be worthy of this cause thereby making this old negro's heart glad and bringing into the lives of his old master and his comrades one of the best Christmas gifts they have ever had.

I shall talk and work for "Dollar Bill's" old soldier friends from now until the subscriptions are closed, and what we do, let's do it now and make this something worthy of the cause.

Yours Truly,
W. L. Williams

In late 1918 at the urging of his many friends, Bill decided to write a small booklet telling the story of his life. When he had completed the short manuscript, he met with the superintendent of the home and explained what he had done. He wanted to sell it for fifteen cents a copy or one dollar and fifty cents per dozen, with all of the money going to the soldier's fund. The superintendent was thrilled and helped Bill get it published. The small, nineteen page booklet was entitled *Bill Yopp "Ten Cent Bill" Narrative of a Slave*. It quickly became a hit with Bill's friends. There were no records kept that showed how much money was raised through the sales of the small book, but it was simply one more gesture on Bill's part that added to his growing legacy.

I'LL SEE YOU UP YONDER

Bill and *The Macon Daily Telegraph* continued with their fundraising project through Christmas of 1919. Each year, the plight of the old soldiers became known by more people throughout the state of Georgia. Hugh Dorsey, the admired governor, had taken up the fight with Bill because it was such a popular cause.

During the Christmases of 1918 and 1919, the governor helped Bill present checks that had grown to over three dollars per soldier. Big photographs of Governor Dorsey and Bill with several of the old soldiers appeared in the Atlanta newspapers. Each time another news story about Bill and his service to the soldiers appeared in the paper, a flood of donations would come directly to the home. The dollars were always divided equally among the men as Bill had wished.

—

In late 1919, at the age of seventy–four, Bill was invited to the state capitol by Governor Dorsey to meet with a group of influential legislators. He was going to promote the need for a pension for the old soldiers in the veterans' home. Before the scheduled meeting, the governor took Bill on a tour of the historic building and introduced him to dozens of lawmakers and other important officials. Bill was pleasantly surprised that they all had heard of him and the work he had been doing on behalf of the soldiers. Once again, he took on the role of being either a novelty or a celebrity. He wasn't sure which. He really didn't care as long as he achieved his goal of helping his friends.

As Bill stepped into the large office where the lawmakers were gathered, all he could think about was how proud his parents and Thomas would be. He said a quick silent prayer and hoped that his parents were watching from above. After an emotional and rousing short speech, the lawmakers gave the diminutive former slave a standing ovation. Soon after, they voted for an annual five hundred dollar pension to be divided among the old soldiers so that they no longer had to rely upon the goodwill of Bill Yopp and the citizens of Georgia.

—

In late December of 1919, Thomas' health took a turn for the worse. He was admitted to the infirmary at the soldier's home. The diagnosis was "old age," and according to his doctor, Thomas was simply worn out from living. Much to Bill's disappointment, Thomas was unable to attend the December Christmas party where Bill presented three dollars to each of the residents of the home. Bill grew increasingly concerned about Thomas as he saw no improvement in his condition. Bill resigned from a part–time job in Atlanta to spend more time with Thomas. Bill moved into the infirmary and spent every waking hour at Thomas' side. His only breaks were to eat, and occasionally he would sleep in an adjoining room. The nurses recounted hearing many late evening chats between Bill and Thomas as they discussed the happier days of their lives. The last public function attended by Thomas was in mid January of 1920. There had been a large birthday celebration for several of the soldiers at the home. Bill, with the help of the kitchen staff, had cooked enough cake for everyone, and Bill insisted that Thomas attend. He felt it would be good for Thomas to see his old friends for what may be his last time. With the assistance of several nurses, Thomas was placed in a wheelchair, and Bill rolled him into the party room where everyone filed past him to shake his hand and wish him well.

On January 23, 1920, at 3:30 in the morning, Captain Thomas Yopp passed away in the infirmary at the soldier's home with Bill sitting by his side, holding his frail hand.

Shortly before Thomas closed his eyes for the final time, he looked into Bill's smiling face and weakly said, "My old friend, I think I have finally come to the end of this long road. I want to thank you for being so kind to me over the years. You have been like a brother to me, and I hold a very special place in my heart for you. My life has been much richer because of you, and I wanted you to know that. And Bill," Thomas said as he weakly took a deep breath, "I asked you back during the war to never call me Master again, but you keep doing it. When you talk about me after I'm gone, just call me Thomas, your friend. You are a much better man than I could ever hope to be. You should be the master."

Bill was so choked up with emotion that he couldn't speak for what seemed like an eternity. Each time he tried to open his mouth he was overcome with sadness.

"Thomas," Bill said, tears reflecting off of his dark cheek in the dim lamplight, "you are the one who made my life better. I know that when you walk through those pearly gates of heaven, the good Lord will thank you for all the kind things you did for my family and me. It has been a wonderful journey, and I'm just happy that we were able to take it together and be together for our final years. I'll see you up yonder before long, and we'll go huntin' and fishin' together again. I'll whistle up the quail just like the old days. I promise."

Bill leaned over and rested his head on Thomas' chest. The two men embraced each other one final time. Minutes later, Bill felt Thomas take his final breath.

Thomas was buried at the vast West View cemetery in Atlanta two days later with full military honors.

—

By that time in Bill's life, his escapades around the world and his work for the Confederate Soldiers Home had drawn so much attention that newspaper stories about him were appearing as far away as New York, California, Nebraska, Canada, and Texas. Shortly after Thomas' death *The New York Times* published a short article about "Ten Cent Bill Yopp" and his dedication to his former master and the old soldiers in Atlanta.

The following newspaper article appeared in dozens

of newspapers across the United States on February 20, 1920.

Former Slave Pays Tribute
Speaks at the Funeral of his Boyhood
Master

There were thirty old veterans from the confederate soldiers' home in H.M. Patterson & Son's chapel. Thursday morning for the double funeral of their comrades, Captain Thomas Mc–Call Yopp and William A. Johnson. There were ladies from the United Daughters of the Confederacy and the Daughters of the American Revolution. There were men from the Grand Army of the Republic. The chapel benches were filled and people stood in the rear. Two ministers spoke—words of honor to the dead and of comfort for the living. A quartet sang and there was prayer.

But it was "one of these whose mission it was to pay the last memorial tribute." The former slave of one of the dead, a man whose heart is as white as his wrinkled face is black, delivered the final funeral oration in the chapel, followed to the cemetery the twin baskets shrouded in the stars and bars, and above the graves at West View bowed his head in pain and love of the master he had served for more than half a century.

"Ten Cent" Bill Yopp, himself, one of the fast–

fading company whose comrades wait for them across the river, was the last and chief to tell these two goodbye. "Ten Cent" Bill, who was "raised" with Captain Yopp in Laurens county, who fished with him and hunted with him as boys together, who –went with him to the wars and fought for him and foraged for him thru four red years, who came back with him to the ruin of his hopes and, tho separated often, never forgot him. Coming each Christmas to the soldiers home in Atlanta, with his words of cheer and gifts for his greatest friend, gifts, too, as time passed, for his friend's friends—"Ten Cent" Bill was servant rather than slave in the old days and more comrade than servant always. It was fitting that he and none other should have preached the Funeral sermon.

He sat, holding his black derby in his hands, his frayed overcoat tightened about his shoulders, on the front row of the chapel. By stretching one hand he could have touched the confederate flag that draped the casket of his master. Behind, him twelve rows were filled with men he had befriended—the thirty veterans from the home. Some of them smiled at him and waved a knotty hand, but, such was the occasion, they were mostly silent in that hushed hour. From the rear you saw thirty pairs of bent shoulders, thirty bowed heads, with wisps of gray making what seemed a gentle halo over each. In the dim light filtering thru the stained glass windows you could see their hands cupped behind their ears, while they listened.

"On the other side of Jordan In the green fields of Eden, Where the Tree of Life is blooming, There is rest for you . . ." The quartet sang, while the listening rows, first strained to catch the words, seemed to relax and be at peace. It was very still as the Rev. R. F. Kirkpatrick, pastor of the West End Presbyterian Church, of which Captain Yopp was a member, prayed. "That there cometh to all of us the Eventide of rest—rest for the weary, was his prayer of thanksgiving, not of sorrow.

Dr. A. R. Holderby, chairman of the home, read from the Bible: "Let not your, heart be troubled," he began. And the verses, so simple and so sure—felt like a quiet hand of comfort. Dr Kirkpatrick spoke of the dead, paying to Captain Yopp his tribute of love and veneration.

When he ended, "Adjutant R. De T. Lawrence, a gentle, white—haired veteran, talked for a moment of his comrades and then introduced "Ten—Cent" Bill who rose in his place and begin to speak. "My dear friends," he said, "I thank you from the depths of my heart for the kind compliment you are paying me and the permission you have given me. I, like the minister who spoke before me, I, too, wish to God that the same old feeling existed today between white and black that existed in 1860. I have known Captain Thomas Mc—Call Yopp, my former master, for sixty– seven years. My mother nursed him, and so his father, who thought so much of him, gave my mother to him before I was born. I know that he never spoke an unkind word to her or any of his servants."

"Since 1854, when I was only a little pickaninny in nothing but a cotton shirt and he wasn't too proud to pick me up and ride me on the back of his horse, we have been friends. We hunted together, and fished together all day long. I rode with him week in and week out We would eat our lunch out in the woods and then come home together. Every night before he would go to bed he would go to one ser- vant's house and to another's and another's, and sit and laugh and joke with them. By and by he would say, 'Bill, I'm getting sleepy,' and we would go back to the big house and eat a little lunch before we went to bed. I slept beside him every night."

"Ten Cent Bill" paused, a gulp in his voice, and then he began to tell of the war, how he and Captain Yopp, joining the army in Atlanta in June 1861, went to Lynchburg in freight cars and took the field. They slept side by side in the Captain's tent, he said, and when it was very bad weather, Captain Yopp, with a single blanket between them, would say, "Cold Bill? Ten…pull over" And Bill would pull. Once Bill was sick and Captain Yopp gave him a pass to Richmond and the money for expenses, Bill leaving only on condition that he could come back.

"He could not see one man imposed on by another," said "Ten–Cent" Bill. "He loved his soldiers equally, as he loved his slaves. He was as brave as a lion and as gentle as a wild flower that grows in the spring. I have been over two–thirds of the world, and I have never known a finer man than Captain Yopp!"

"If his funeral were being held today in Laurens county," continued "Ten–Cent" Bill, "the streets would not hold the people. Only a thin veil separates life from death. He had pierced that veil, but we shall join him soon. Death, has taken charge of his body, but I know that God has taken charge of his soul!"

"Ten–Cent" Bill stopped, his head bowed, his hand raised, and with that benediction, the audience stirred and began to file out.

Immediately following Bill's final Christmas speech to the old soldiers in 1920, the superintendent of the home told everyone to remain seated in the chapel because he and the members of the Board of Trustees had a special presentation. A dozen of Atlanta's most prominent citizens and politicians came forward and stood at the front of the chapel. Major McAllister introduced them all.

"Bill," McAllister said, "would you please step back up here for a minute?"

With a surprised look on his face, Bill rose from his

chair rather slowly, shuffled to the front of the room, and stood by Major McAllister.

"Bill, on behalf of the Board of Trustees of the home and all of the men who live here, we have a special gift for you to show our thanks and appreciation for the countless hours you have worked on behalf of the home and the soldiers. Today we are issuing a special invitation, unlike anything we have ever done, for you to move into the home and live out the remainder of your life with your friends. We have already made arrangements for you to have the same room that your friend, Thomas Yopp, lived in for so many years. We think he would be very pleased, as are we, that you will be the first colored man who has ever been given a place in any Confederate Soldiers' Home. Certainly no one deserves it more than you." McAllister paused and smiled. "And also Bill, the men of the home have asked me to give you a very special gift from them. They have been working on this for some time. They took up a collection and had this made to show their appreciation and love for you."

McAllister took a small, highly polished leather box from the pulpit and opened it. He reached in and removed a stunning gold medal that hung on a red, white, and blue ribbon. On the medal was an engraved picture of a Confederate drummer boy, and on the back were these words: *To Bill Yopp from your friends at the Georgia Confederate Soldiers' Home. You have helped us through many battles.* The crowded room broke out into wild applause and cheers. Bill was choked with emotion. He stood on the steps beside the pulpit, shook McAllister's hand, and then bowed to the audience to show his thanks. He then removed his handkerchief and began wiping his eyes and clearing his throat. He was speechless.

———

Soon after that momentous night, Bill moved into Thomas' old room and began the next stage of his life. He continued with his daily work of helping anyone in need at the home and doing whatever he could to improve the quality of life of the residents. Once again, just like his days in the army, he found himself doing the things for his comrades that he truly enjoyed. He read books to the men who could not read or were too blind to see the words. He wrote letters to their families for them. He took men for walks and exercise. Whenever a soldier was depressed, Bill would magically appear in his room to brighten his day. Most importantly, he knew every man by name and was always there when needed.

It was common practice at the veterans' home that most able–bodied men were given jobs either at the home or in the nearby community. These jobs were intended to enhance their sense of well–being, as well as put a few extra dollars into their pockets. Shortly after Thomas died, the governor of Georgia arranged a job for Bill at the state capitol, where he served as a messenger for the Speaker of the House during legislative sessions. Bill's uncanny memory and kind nature served him well in the position, and he was always greeted warmly when he entered the offices of the powerful government officials. Bill served in that capacity until he was nearly ninety years old.

—

On June 3, 1936, one month before Bill's ninety–first birthday, one of Bill's friends walked into his room and found that he had passed away while sitting in his rocking chair. His head rested comfortably on the back of the chair, his eyes were closed, and a peaceful smile was on his lips. As usual, he was wearing a crisp white shirt and tie, his ever present black suit, and his shoes shining like new. In his coat pocket, in clear view, was the gold writing pen that had been given to him so many years earlier by Mr. Brown in Macon. On a small table near his chair was the gold medal given to him by his friends at the home and the gold pocket watch given to him by the officers at Camp Wheeler. It was fitting that Bill was admiring these wonderful tokens of appreciation when he closed his eyes for the final time.

—

As a final tribute to a great man, the State of Georgia voted that Bill should be buried with full military honors in the Confederate Cemetery in Marietta, Georgia. He was the only black soldier ever laid to rest in the vast graveyard of over three thousand forgotten heroes.

And perhaps, just perhaps, the most fitting thing of all was that they chose to bury him on the front row,

where the drummer boy belonged. There was little do
that this had been his destiny all along.

THE GREATEST LESSON OF THEM ALL

JUNE 7, 1936
CONFEDERATE MILITARY CEMETERY
MARIETTA, GEORGIA

The musket blasts from the Confederate honor guard shattered the peaceful silence of the cemetery and woke several of the elderly soldiers from their daydreams. The seven soldiers pointed their guns toward the sky, fired, and then reloaded until twenty-one shots had been delivered for the standard salute to a fallen hero. The thick white clouds of drifting smoke from the rifles nearly obscured the soldiers and the mourners.

When the ceremony finished, small groups of mourners and dignitaries began milling around. Some walked up to the flag draped casket and touched it with soft hands of honor and sympathy. Others stood off in the background and watched in silence. A well-dressed black family walked up the hill toward the casket. A father, mother, and six children ranging in ages stopped near the flag draped casket. The black man removed his Sunday hat and spoke to his children.

"This is your great-great-uncle whom we came all this way to pay our respects to, children," he said softly. "He was a wonderful man, and I hope each of you can learn something from his life that will make you a better person."

"I never got to meet Bill," the father continued, "but I heard lots of wonderful stories about him from my grandmother before she died several years back."

The father looked down at his youngest son and kneeled beside him.

"Son, since you have been named for Bill Yopp, you have a big responsibility to live up to the name he made for himself and for our family."

The six year old boy shuffled his feet, looked his father in the eyes, and replied, "Yes sir. I know all about Uncle Bill, and I'll be as good a boy as he was. I promise."

As the black family turned to leave the gravesite, each one of them took a shiny new dime from their pockets and placed it on the casket to honor Bill's legacy.

The young boy named Bill was last in line, and after placing his dime and walking several steps, he turned back to the casket and waved.

"Goodbye, Ten Cent Bill. Have a fun time in heaven with Thomas."

EPILOGUE

uring February and March of 2008, several events occurred that are extremely important to the legacy of Bill Yopp.

First, a number of people have recently come forward stating that they are descendants of Bill Yopp. Prior to this, I had been unable to confirm with certainty any of Bill's relatives. Based on this revelation, I have spent countless hours attempting to trace these lines in a search for the actual names of Bill's parents. I recently discovered that in the 1870 census in Laurens County, a William Yopp, Sr. (age forty, born in South Carolina in 1830) was married to Helia (who I referred to as Lia in the story), and living next door was William Yopp, Jr. (age twenty–two) with Anna. I have been unable to confirm with complete certainty that this William Jr. is our "Ten Cent Bill," but it appears to be him based upon other compelling circumstantial evidence. For future Yopp genealogists, I must restate that I do not have 100% confirmation that William Sr. and Helia are Bill Yopp's parents. However, they are the most likely candidates.

Next, I have recently discovered conflicting reports as to whether Bill Yopp was actually with Company H at Appomattox when Lee surrendered. Most Civil War research shows that he was present and on the roster in Virginia at that time. However, I recently came across some sketchy information based on documents from the Confederate Soldier's Home in Atlanta stating that Bill was on furlough in Laurens County, Georgia, at the time of Lee's surrender. I continue to investigate this and hope to find the truth one day.

And finally, on March 5, 2008, Bill Yopp received what is perhaps his greatest honor. The governor of the State of Georgia, Sonny Perdue, proclaimed the date as "Bill Yopp Day" as a tribute to his numerous accomplishments. Several of Bill's relatives, along with various legislators and notable historians, attended the event at the Georgia State Capitol. I was honored to be invited to attend this event, which also included a touching ceremony at Bill's grave in the Confederate Cemetery in Marietta, Georgia. The overall proclamation and event was promoted as part of "Confederate History Month" in the state of Georgia.

—

As the visitors slowly departed the vast military cemetery, I remained behind until they all were gone. I was alone with Bill and the thousands of soldiers who rested on this quiet hill. After several minutes of silent reflection, I stepped up to Bill's small tombstone, placed a shiny new dime on it, and said thanks to Ten Cent Bill for sharing his remarkable life with me.

Confederate Soldier's Home, Atlanta, Georgia, 1915
Courtesy of The Macon Telegraph.

Bill Yopp 1915,
Courtesy of The Macon
Telegraph.

CAPTAIN YOPP,
TEN-CENT BILL'S OLD MASTER, WHO LATELY DIED AT
SOLDIERS HOME.

Captain Thomas Yopp shortly before he died in 1921.
Courtesy of The Macon Telegraph.

Bill Yopp Gives his Master, Thomas Yopp, a pie in 1920.
Courtesy of The Macon Telegraph.

Georgia Governor Dorsey assists Bill Yopp with distributing
$3.00 to each man at the Soldier's Home in 1919.
Courtesy of The Macon Telegraph.

Bill Yopp Distributes Cash from his fund to Veterans at the Soldier's home 1919.

Courtesy of The Macon Telegraph.

Poster of "City of New York" steamship that Bill returned from Europe on after his visit in 1889.

USS Brutus, US Navy ship that Bill spent many years on and traveled around the world.

Bill Yopp's grave marker in Confederate Cemetery, Marietta, Georgia. Grave marker reads "Drummer, Bill Yopp, Company H, 14th Ga. Infantry, CSA."
Courtesy of David McPheeters, Snellville, Georgia, 2007.

Georgia Governor Sonny Purdue proclaims March 5, 2008, as
Bill Yopp Day. Attending were several of Bill Yopp's relatives
and the author, Charles Pittman.

BIBLIOGRAPHY

Scott B. Thompson, Sr., *"Ten–Cent" Bill Yopp*, http://organizations.nlamerica.com/hardy/MilitaryHistory/TenCent.html

Forgotten Confederates, *Roster of Confederate Soldiers of Georgia*, Confederate Veteran, Volume XXVIII (1920),

Scott W. Warren, *Muster roll of Company H, 14th Regiment CSA*, http://ftp.rootsweb.com/pub/usgenweb/ga/laurens/military/civilwar/14thregh.txt

Charles W. Hampton. *Bill Yopp "Ten Cent Bill" A Narrative Of A Slave!* vClarkston, Georgia, 1969

R. de T. Lawrence, *The History of Bill Yopp*, Atlanta, Ga., 1920;

The New York Times, *Died, Attended by Ex–Slave*, January 25, 1920 (no author shown)

The New York Times, *Negro Plays Santa to Old Confederates*, December 25, 1919 (no author shown)

"The Confederate Veteran," Nov/Dec., 1992, pp. 12 – 15,

Macon Daily Telegraph, *Ante–Bellum Negro "Ten–cent Bill" Finds Old Master in Soldier's Home*, Macon, Georgia, October 27, 1917 page 1–A

Macon Daily Telegraph, *Negro (Yopp) Starts Fund to Make Master of 60's Happy Again*, Macon, Georgia, October 28, 1918, page 1–A

Macon Daily Telegraph, *Ten–Cent Bill's Fund is Growing*, Macon, Georgia, October 30, 1918, page 1–A

Macon Daily Telegraph, *Veterans in Home to Be Remembered*, Macon, Georgia, November 2, 1918, page 1–A

Macon Daily Telegraph, *Silver Dollar Sent in U.S. Mail for Georgia Veterans*, Macon, Georgia, November 4, 1918, page 1–A

Macon Daily Telegraph, *Ten–Cent Bill's Fund is Climbing*, Macon, Georgia, November 6, 1918, page 1–A

Macon Daily Telegraph, *More than $100 in Ten–Cent Bill Fund*, Macon, Georgia, November 7, 1918, page 12–A

Macon Daily Telegraph, *Ten Cent Bill Makes His Last Appeal for Vets' Yuletide Fund*, Macon, Georgia, November 9, 1919, page 1–A

Macon Daily Telegraph, *Ten–Cent Bill Goes to Atlanta Today To Cheer Vets*, Macon, Georgia, December 18, 1919, page 1–A

Evening State Journal and Lincoln Daily News," *Former Slave Pays Tribute,*

Speaks at the Funeral of his Boyhood Master" February 20, 1920, PAGE 9, Lincoln, Nebraska

Macon Daily Telegraph, *Bill Raises $275 for Old Soldiers; Old Negro Will Carry Money Offered to Gladden Season for Vets*, Macon, Georgia, December 19, 1919, page 1–A

Macon Daily Telegraph, *"Ten–Cent Bill" Gives "Confeds" Christmas Cheer*, Macon, Georgia, December 21, 1919, page 1–A

Confederate Soldiers' Home Publication, *"In Memory of the Heroes in Gray"*, 1934, page 49

The Dublin Courier Herald, *"Bill Yopp Here…Laurens County Negro Known all over State"*, November, 1924. (story outlines Bill's involvement as messenger in State Legislature)

Department Of The Navy—naval Historical Center, USS *Brutus* (AC–15), 1898–1922, http://www.history.navy.mil/photos/sh–usn/usnsh–b/brutus.htm

"City of Paris" and "City of New York", Twin Screw Steamers of the Inman Line, promotional poster. (Ships Bill took to and from Europe in 1899)

Death Certificate Of Thomas M. Yopp, *Georgia's Virtual Vault*, online historical death certificates. http://content.sos.state.ga.us/cdm4/item_viewer.php?CISOROOT=/gadeaths&CISOPTR=51782&CISOBOX=1&REC=2

listen|imagine|view|experience

AUDIO BOOK DOWNLOAD INCLUDED WITH THIS BOOK!

In your hands you hold a complete digital entertainment package. Besides purchasing the paper version of this book, this book includes a free download of the audio version of this book. Simply use the code listed below when visiting our website. Once downloaded to your computer, you can listen to the book through your computer's speakers, burn it to an audio CD or save the file to your portable music device (such as Apple's popular iPod) and listen on the go!

How to get your free audio book digital download:

1. Visit www.tatepublishing.com and click on the e|LIVE logo on the home page.
2. Enter the following coupon code:
   6970-d2f2-ce54-c2df-f417-03a8-fa6b-d88a
3. Download the audio book from your e|LIVE digital locker and begin enjoying your new digital entertainment package today!